500 Words or Less

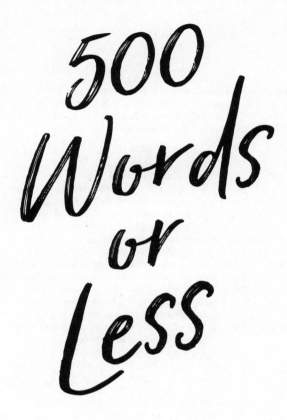

500 Words or Less

JULEAH DEL ROSARIO

SIMON PULSE

New York   London   Toronto   Sydney   New Delhi

SIMON PULSE

An imprint of Simon & Schuster Children's Publishing Division
1230 Avenue of the Americas, New York, New York 10020
First Simon Pulse hardcover edition September 2018
Text copyright © 2018 by Juleah Swanson
Jacket illustration copyright © 2018 by Cannaday Chapman
For information about special discounts for bulk purchases, please contact
Simon & Schuster Special Sales at 1-866-506-1949 or business@simonandschuster.com.
The Simon & Schuster Speakers Bureau can bring authors to your live event.
For more information or to book an event contact the Simon & Schuster Speakers
Bureau at 1-866-248-3049 or visit our website at www.simonspeakers.com.
Jacket designed by Sarah Creech
Interior designed by Mike Rosamilia
The text of this book was set in Iowan Old Style.
Manufactured in the United States of America
2 4 6 8 10 9 7 5 3 1
Library of Congress Cataloging-in-Publication Data
Names: Del Rosario, Juleah, author.
Title: 500 words or less / Juleah del Rosario.
Other titles: Five hundred words or less
Description: First Simon Pulse hardcover edition. | New York : Simon Pulse, 2018. |
Summary: High school senior Nic, seventeen, tries to salvage her tattered reputation
by helping her Ivy League–obsessed classmates with college admission essays and finds
herself in the process.
Identifiers: LCCN 2017048137 | ISBN 9781534410442 (hardcover)
Subjects: | CYAC: Novels in verse. | Identity—Fiction. | High schools—Fiction. |
Schools—Fiction. | Dating (Social customs)—Fiction. | Family problems—Fiction. |
Racially mixed people—Fiction. | Chinese Americans—Fiction.
Classification: LCC PZ7.5.D45 Aah 2018 | DDC [Fic]—dc23
LC record available at https://lccn.loc.gov/2017048137
ISBN 9781534410466 (eBook)

To my sister,
for all the times you said,
"Let's read."

PART I:
Rejection

This was senior year
Someone had written WHORE
in bright orange lipstick
on my locker.

It was waiting for me
after third period,
like an old friend
                    hanging

around after class.

For the past three weeks,
I have filed down these halls,
opened this locker,
stuffed textbooks
and slightly damp rain jackets inside.

I've regurgitated facts,
aced exams,
daydreamed about life
at an Ivy like Princeton,

and sometimes I've thought
about Ben.

It was life in a holding pattern,
circling around an airport
where you can't yet land.

I glanced over to Jordan's locker
and saw its pristine state.
No bright orange lipstick.

Was there even a male equivalent
to the word "whore"?

There were words,
but none that carried
the same weight.

Maybe I would have cried
if I were
a different girl.

But this was senior year,
and my life was more than
a series of letters
scrawled on a locker, vying
to break me.

This happened once before

Two years ago,
shortly after my mother
disappeared.

I tried
scrubbing the lipstick
off with toilet paper.

Tiny bits of tissue
crumbled in my hand,
but the letters remained intact.

Two years ago
Jordan was there.
"Who did this?" he demanded.

Two years ago
Ben was there.
"My girlfriend's not
a whore," he said.

They both hulked out,
pacing in front of my locker.

When the bell rang
and students streamed into the hallway,

Jordan and Ben glared
at each and every one of them
who dared to glance
in my direction.

"Hey, ass face,
you think my girlfriend's a whore?"
Ben assaulted a freshman.

"Guys. Knock it off.
Somebody go get
a wet paper towel."

Jordan obeyed.
Ben stood by my side.

"Why would someone
write that?" he said.

"Don't worry about it.
It's probably a mistake,"
I said, but

I thought about my mother,
and the women
who whispered
about her.

I thought about the words
they used in replacement
of her name,
words that were never meant
to be associated with someone
I called "Mom."

If my mother had known
what people were saying
behind her back,
if she had known
what someone would write
on *my* locker,
would she have left?

I wondered if the rumors
were true
about my mom,
and people my classmates
called "Dad."

I wondered
who else believed
these rumors.

I wondered
what

people believed
about me.

But what can you do
when someone writes WHORE
on your locker,
except wipe away the lipstick

and move on.

This time
It wasn't a mistake.

This time
I didn't have Ben or Jordan
around
to defend my honor.

This time
I armed myself
with a dampened
paper towel and scrubbed
fruitlessly.

A green glob
landed on my locker
and dribbled down the front.

Behind me
a boy
held out a bottle
of dish soap.

"Do you always carry that around?"
I asked.

Green goop mingled
with the lipstick.
Letters began to fade.

"Don't question. Just thank me."
He held out a dry paper towel.

"Thanks?"
I returned to scrubbing.
The lipstick slid off easily.

"Girl, you of all people should know
that a wet paper towel
isn't gonna remove
a petroleum-based lipstick."

"Huh?"
I stopped scrubbing.

"Last year
you were the top student
in AP Chemistry.

"You beat me
by .25 percentage points."

He handed me
another paper towel.
"And I'm damn good
at chemistry."

I should have known
his name,

but at some point I stopped
paying attention
to details that didn't matter
for GPAs and college admissions.

"Why are you
an expert
on removing lipstick
from lockers?"
I asked.

"My sister used to think
it was *so hilarious*
to use lipstick
on my car window,
as if writing from a supposed
secret admirer.

"That shit ain't funny."

He squirted more dish soap
onto the locker.
"Lipstick is a bitch
to clean off."

I opened my mouth
to say something snarky
but stopped.

"Thanks," I said quietly.

He glanced down at his watch.
"I've gotta get to class."

The bell rang five minutes ago.
"What are you still doing here?"
I asked.

"Dunno," he said,
and walked away.

To the last period of the day
I was early,
but so was half the class,
already seated,
with textbooks out, because
we were nerds who liked to get crackin'
on mitochondria and mitosis.

Someone was in my seat.

That guy,
the one with the dish soap.

He wore fluorescent orange sneakers,
with two silver stripes,
like a safety cone.

"You're in my seat," I said.

"Nope. It's my seat now."

The boy nodded
toward words
on a screen
that read
"New seating assignments."

Projected above
the best seat in the class
was the name
"Ashok."

Ashok, I repeated.

He looked up at me.
"Yeah?"

Shit.
I didn't mean
to say it out loud.

"Do you ever go
by a nickname,
like Ash?"
I tried to recover.

"Why would I go by Ash?
That sounds like
a white boy's name."

"I have a white boy's name," I said.

He snorted. "That you do, Nic,
but you're also not white,

and you're not a boy.
So you just have
a weird name
like me."

"Okay, Ashok."
I hovered over his seat.
"Tell me where I'm supposed to sit."

He scanned the air with his finger
and motioned to the desk next to him.
"Welcome, neighbor."

I slumped into
the subpar seat.

Jordan Parker
Entered class
with his hand raised.

"Who can describe for me the process
of embryological development?"
our AP Bio teacher asked.
We looked down at our textbooks,
flipping through pages
for an answer.

"The embryological development process
begins with fertilization
where an egg is fertilized by a sperm
and a zygote is formed,"
Jordan said.

"Mr. Parker, answering this question
does not excuse
your tardiness."

Jordan raised a finger
and pulled a piece of paper
out of his back pocket.

Our teacher shook his head.
"Okay, fine," he said.

Juleah del Rosario

"Please take your seat in front of"—
he scanned the room, his gaze landing
on the empty desk in front of me—
"Ms. Chen."

Jordan saw the empty seat.

"Of course,"
we both muttered.

You racist
Jordan leaned back in his chair,
imposing on my desk space.
"Can you help me with my homework
for Japanese?" he whispered.

"I've never taken Japanese, Jordan."

I didn't know why
Jordan was talking to me
now
after weeks
of silence.

"But you speak it, right?"

"You know I'm part Chinese, Jordan."

I didn't know why
Jordan needed
anyone's help
with anything
other than
the quality
of his character.

"It's like the same thing—
Chinese, Japanese, Korean,"
Jordan said.

I couldn't see his face,
but I imagined
a sheepish grin
with arrogant eyes
that still read,
Ben doesn't go here
anymore,

like it was
all on
me.

I kicked his seat
hard.
Jordan lunged forward,
laughing.

"I only know Spanish, you racist," I said.

The class turned in our direction.
Jordan stifled a laugh.

I felt my face burn
like a house to the ground.

But I raised my hand
to answer
the next question
on ectoderm
and mesoderm
and endoderm.

I was still going to be
the girl
who aced
this goddamn class.

Lifetimes ago
It was just the three of us,
Jordan, Ben, and me,
friends—
not lovers or enemies.

When I was little,
I didn't understand dolls.
I didn't like dressing things up
and forcing plastic toys
with shiny blond hair
to drink tea
or go on dates
or drive around in a pink Corvette.
I liked hanging out with Jordan and Ben.

We stood around Jordan's backyard,
the three of us in our rain slickers.
Jordan would hand each of us a shovel.
"Today we're digging to China,"
he would say.

Then he would turn to me,
"You can visit your relatives."

Ben would start digging,
always the loyal sidekick.

I knew better.
"This is ridiculous, Jordan.
It's impossible
to dig to China."

Jordan would shake his head.
"What's ridiculous is not trying, Nic.
How do we know what's possible
if we don't try?"

"Science," I would mumble.
"Science tells us this is impossible."

But in spite of my protests,
I'd pick up a shovel
and start digging straight into the corner
of the Parkers' perfectly manicured lawn,
because
maybe today
it wasn't so

impossible.

Juleah del Rosario

Tires screeching #2

Jordan Parker's Range Rover
idled
behind my parked car
after seventh period.

A blond sophomore hung
on to the window
like a lemur,
her eyes big and black
and foolish
like a lemur's.

I laid on my horn.
The sophomore turned around
and glared.

Jordan leaned closer
to the wheel.
He waved with his fingers,
as if to say "Toodles" or "Cheerio."

"Move your fucking car!"
I yelled
out the driver's-side window.

He flashed a smile.
"Jesus, Nicky.
Don't get your panties in a bunch."

I thought about the sound
of metal against metal,
of black paint
chipping off a shiny exterior,
of the shrill screams and obscenities
that would follow
if I acted upon
what I saw in my head.

I kept it in neutral.

"It's Nic.
My name is Nic, Jordan.
Not Nicky," I yelled back.
You of all people should know this,
I wanted to say.

There was a time when I was a Nic to Jordan,
like one of his buddies,
not Nicky,
like one of his conquests.

Jordan's mouth curled slightly,
knowingly.
Then he continued on
with his business
with the lemur.

I slumped back,
watching the two of them flirt
through the rearview mirror.

With one final toss
of her hair,
the sophomore hopped
into the SUV.

They sped away,
tires screeching around a corner.

I hated that sound.
It gave me that feeling
in the pit of my stomach
that's not quite nausea
but not quite
not.

That sound
reminded me
of Ben.

Juleah del Rosario

Ben moved away
And I felt so empty.

I missed him so much,

like the feeling of forgetting a sweater
in the middle of winter,

like the feeling of having no one to sit with
in a crowded cafeteria,

like the feeling
of being restless,
and so deeply alone.

Almost every part of me wanted him back.
The heart, the skin,
the tired and achy muscles.
But my rational brain kept telling me
what an idiot I was
for thinking that it would ever
come true.

There already was
an end,
between Ben
and me.

Except
there was a place
in my broken heart
where possibility still remained.

Hope sat
On a back burner,
in a teakettle,
warming
but never boiling.

Never screaming.
Never wailing.
Only mildly percolating.

Rumbling just enough
to remind me
of possibilities,
of hope.

"How was school?"
Was one of those questions
that adults asked
just to get you talking.
"It was fine," I would say to Xiaoling
every afternoon when I arrived home
from school.

My stepmother would shuffle around
the kitchen and make me a snack,
neither of us saying
anything more.

When Mom was around,
she didn't ask me questions.
She already knew all the answers.

"I heard
that Jenny and Jordan
are dating."

"The winter formal is coming up.
You should go."

"I don't understand
why Meydenbauer parents
condone sending their children

on unsupervised
spring break trips to Cabo.
You're not going."

When Mom was around,
she knew the names of my classmates,
she knew all their mothers,
and she knew of the gossip
that spread around town.

But it wasn't what happened in Cabo
that any of the mothers cared about.

It was the rumors
of covert affairs,
of cheating husbands,
and of the woman
who they saw
as "the other."

Without Mom
there were no more answers,
nor questions either.

At least, not questions
I wanted to ask anyone
out loud.

Xiaoling

I loved Xiaoling, though
not like a mother.
She didn't pretend
to be my mom.

She tiptoed around the issue of discipline
and turned the other way when I turned up
at ten a.m. on a Sunday morning.

I wondered if Xiaoling was happy
here in America,
with us,
with my dad.

I wondered if she thought she made the right
decision,
to pack her bags,
her son,
her life,
and fly business class to America
to marry a strange, short but successful
software engineer.

I wondered if she loved my dad,
if she saw something in him
that Mom and I
did not.

Dinner

Dad drank
Chianti with his
Szechuan-style steak.

He savored every second.

I sat there
with a polished-off plate
watching Xiaoling pour
Dad another glass.

Silence smothered the table.
It choked the air.
It felt lonelier
than being alone.

Mom never made us
sit at this table.

Dad wafted the fresh pour.
He set down the wine,
and then he said,
"How are your grades?"

"They're still As,"
I said,

moving the tines of a fork
across oil slicks and streaks of sauce
on an otherwise
white plate.

He slowly chewed
his steak
and said,
"Senior year counts.
Make sure
they stay
that way."

If my body could dive
into a pile of textbooks
and swim around
and surface at the end
of the year
with straight As
wrung from my body,

then maybe I could be
the perfect daughter to Dad
and Xiaoling.

But I could feel
the parts of Mom

that slid over my shoulders
seeped into my skin,
sat in this chair,

restless
under a Chihuly sculpture
that she selected.

Like a fine wine
When I told my dad
I was applying early
decision to Princeton,

he responded with
"Very good selection,"
as if I had ordered
a fine bottle of wine.

Mom poured herself another
From a bottle of chardonnay
on one of the last nights
before she disappeared.

I side-eyed her behavior,
but she didn't notice.

She's stopped noticing
a lot of things.

Like how much
I wanted her
to be the mom
who couldn't
French braid
my hair
because she sucked
at it,
not the mom
who couldn't
French braid
my hair
because she was
drunk.

She teetered over to the table
cast in orange light.

"What are you working on?"
"Trig," I grunted.
She swirled her glass.
"I can help you with that," she said brightly.

"I know. But I've got this."
I scratched out another answer.

"When I was your age . . ."
"Mom." I pointed to the textbook
and reached for a pair of earbuds.

She caught my hand.
Her skin felt raw.
"Let me sit here with you.
I promise
I'll be quiet."

I pulled away from her.
"Fine."

Rain smattered against the windows
and drizzled down the drainpipe.

And an hour later, Mom prattled away
about the gossip at the tennis club.
The recent divorcée dating a younger man.
"Twenty-five."
The hair color of the saleswoman
at Nordstrom.
"Silver with lavender hues."
Mom mused
about whether she should go back
to grad school.
Finish the dissertation
she never started.
Or maybe learn how to code.
"I could work for a start-up, Nic."

She was like the evening news,
the hum of a steady voice,
drowning against the sound of rain.

I finished all thirty problems in trig
and moved on to US History.

Dad came home at midnight.
His eyes glazed over Mom
slumped in a chair
and an empty bottle of wine.

"Did you finish your homework?"
"Just did," I said.
He nodded. "Get some sleep.
It's a school night."
He padded back down the hall.

"I can drive you to school tomorrow,"
Mom mumbled.

I packed away my notebooks
and kissed her on the forehead.
"Go to bed," I whispered,
and she reached for my hand
and squeezed it.

In my room I texted Kitty.
Can I get a ride in the morning?

It's already morning,
she texted back.

Kitty texted me

Twice
during the awkward
family dinner.

Ohmygod. Ohmy
God. My parents are letting
me out of the house.

And

The twins are throwing
a party. Please, please
say you'll go.

An hour later,
with Kitty's persistence,
I found my way
into an outfit.

I looked like a girl
taking a last stand
on summer.

A cotton shirt
that slipped down my shoulder.

Juleah del Rosario

Boy shorts and Rainbows.
A single messy braid
and a makeupless face except for
the dark smudges of eyeliner
outlined over and over again.

"Hot" is all
Kitty said
as she took one look
at me and headed to the car.

Kitty drove
in six-inch heels,
and a miniskirt
that was more mini
than skirt.

"Kitty, seriously,
can you even drive?"

She rolled her eyes.
"Of course I can.
I'm an awesome driver.
I aced my driver's test,
and I was wearing
these same shoes."

I worried about all
the poor choices
I had made,
including getting into this car
with Kitty.

"Why would you wear those
to your driver's test?"

Kitty shrugged. "Because they were new."

On not being best friends

If I were thirteen and had to give
one half of a "best friend" necklace,
a broken heart with

be

fri

on one half and

st

end

on the other,
then obviously I'd give it to Kitty.
She was more than a best friend.

But Kitty had an actual best friend.
Her name was Sarah.
Kitty and Sarah have lived next door
to each other
their whole lives,
so I guess that made them
best friends.

Sarah was one year older than us.
So now she's in college
at Sarah Lawrence.
Sarah went to Sarah Lawrence.

I mean, it's a common name
and it's a good school, but
who does that?

Like, were there any Stanfords
at Stanford?

How many Sarahs
attended Sarah Lawrence?
Was it higher than average?
Were there more Sarahs per capita
at Sarah Lawrence
than at any other school?

I tried to be friends with Sarah,
but we didn't click,
not in the same way
that Kitty and I clicked.

Maybe it was because
Kitty and I
were opposites.

Kitty was a constant bundle
of nervous energy.

Juleah del Rosario

It wasn't usually noticeable until
it was quiet,
and then she was a constant buzz,
like an appliance.

If Kitty were to describe me

She would say, "Nic has black hair
that sometimes smells like a fruit smoothie."
Actually, no, it's not black.
It has reddish highlights
and walnut lowlights,
the kind of color that women pay
two hundred dollars
to achieve.

If Nic were an animal, she'd be a gazelle.
She has an elegance
like a dancer, and maybe
if she didn't hate leotards and pink tights
she would have turned into one.

(Okay, maybe Kitty wouldn't compare me to
a gazelle.
Maybe she'd say I'm more like
an inchworm,
calculated, precise, inconsequential.)

I knew what Kitty would definitely say,
though, because
she was obsessed, in a slightly

politically incorrect
kind of way,
with my genetic makeup.

She'd say that Nic was one of those girls,
who was clearly only half-Asian,
because she looked
less than 100 percent White, and
less than 100 percent Chinese.

She'd say I'm lucky because
half-Asians were always prettier than
white girls like her.

I'd say, "Not always. Remember Tory
in second grade?
She was funny-looking,
and not in a good way."

Kitty would wrinkle her nose
and give me a look.

"Everyone has beauty, Nic."

Kitty's first party

Jenny Pugh—one half of the Pugh twins—
wore a strapless gold dress
that clung to all the wrong curves.

She marched toward us,
clomping her Louboutins
across the marble floor.

"Oh, you're here."
Jenny smelled sweet,
like lilacs and cotton candy
and a pitcher of margaritas.

I smiled on the outside.
"Thanks for the invite."

"I didn't invite you," Jenny replied.
She glanced over at Kitty
as if the words extended to her
by default.

"I know," I said.
I stood unflinching,
but part of me
already wanted
to leave.

But this was Kitty's first party,
and she didn't deserve to be ostracized
just because she was
loyal and kind
and friends with me.

Jenny huffed.
"Why are you here?
After what you did
to Ben.
He transferred to Prep,
you know."

The red Solo cup tipped
precariously in her hand.
It smelled fruity
and flammable.

Of course I knew.
I tried calling and texting
after Jordan's party.
I waited by my phone, hoping
that every
single
text
would be
from Ben.

They never were.

I drove to Ben's house
and saw a moving truck
haul away his family's belongings.
I saw an agent ram a FOR SALE sign
into the lawn.

Ben no longer went
to Meydenbauer, but
he wasn't a million miles away.

He was living at an estate
that his mother inherited
somewhere on the edge
of town.

The move had been planned
for months, but
I didn't think it was possible
with all the technology around us
for someone to disappear
so easily
from our lives.

But with Ben,
I guess it wasn't that hard.

Juleah del Rosario

To Ben,
I no longer existed.

"He won't even return my texts."
Jenny pouted.

"You and me both,"
I said.

Jenny was not amused.
"Who the hell transfers schools
before their senior year?"

"It was his parents," Kitty said.
"They thought he would have
a better shot at an Ivy."
Kitty shrugged, as if to say,
Wouldn't you have done the same?

"But the kids at Prep
are freaks,"
Jenny said.

Ben left the circles of friends
he held together.
He abandoned sports teams.
He resigned from student government.

He walked away from everyone,
but he drove away from me.

Jenny scoffed
and glared at me

until her twin sister, Audrey,
wobbled down a grand staircase
slurring indiscernible words,
at a very discernible volume.

"How will Audrey ever survive
college without me?"
Jenny muttered,
clomping her way
to her twin.

I grabbed Kitty by the arm.
"Let's go find the drinks."

I navigated our way around
a huddle of senior girls
who loitered in the living room.

Kitty waved at all of them.
A few half smiled in return.
But as I walked by,

they lowered their voices;
they tightened their circle.
They all averted their eyes.

I imagined the thought bubbles
that hovered over their heads.
I thought maybe I would see
screams and taunts
and flashes of obscenities.

But when the girls
glanced back up,
all I could see
were eight eyes blinking
beneath an empty bubble
because there was nothing
left to say.

I was the ghost
of my former self
who most people
saw right through.

We found handles
Of cheap vodka, rum, and whiskey
wafting toxic smells
on the kitchen counter.

"What do you want?"
I said to Kitty.

Her eyes grew wide.
"Anything. I can have anything?"

"Anything that can be mixed
with what's here."

I waved my hand across
a garden variety of mixers—
Diet Coke, Red Bull,
Cran-Apple juice, Crystal Light,
and a bottle of organic soda,
flavor unknown.

Kitty started pouring
everything—
and I mean everything,
including the dredges of empty bottles—
into a plastic cup.

"What are you doing?"
I said.

"It's my Kitty drink!"

"It's a suicide,"
I said.

She shrugged, holding up her cup,
admiring the concoction for a moment
before taking a large gulp.

Then she coughed
and sputtered
and said,
"I think it needs more Diet Coke."

I nodded apprehensively.
"I think you'd better hand over your keys."

Kitty nodded willingly.
"Okay. You're the expert
on these things."

"An expert
on parties

or on alcohol?"
I asked.

She took another gulp
but didn't answer.

I didn't want
to be considered
an expert on either.

Both left me
with an aftertaste
that felt like sadness.

I poured myself
a generous cup full
of mystery-flavored
organic soda
and pocketed
Kitty's keys.

What happens at a Meydenbauer party

"Now what?" Kitty asked.

"You're pretty much
 looking at it."

Through the sliding glass door,
guys in fluorescent tanks
with unwavering concentration
battled it out over
a game of beer pong.

The coffee table
in front of a flat-screen
had been removed
to make room
for a dance floor.

Sophomore and junior girls
were going fucking nuts
dancing
to R. Kelly's "Ignition (Remix),"

while a couch full of guys
from the JV football team
sat on a sectional and stared.

"It feels so wrong
to love this song
so much,"
Kitty griped,
and belted out the lyrics.

I was about to deconstruct
our love for "Ignition"
as the ultimate form
of privilege,

but then I saw
Jordan Parker
leaning against a wall
paying attention to
no one, yet surrounded
by everyone who mattered
to the social structure
of Meydenbauer.

He didn't have to say
the right things.

He didn't have to pretend
to like people.

He didn't have to wear

Ray-Bans or Chuck Taylors,
or fluorescent-colored anything,

because the way he wore
his arrogance
was enough
to attract
his admirers.

Then a sophomore
doubled over
and puked
on the hardwood floor
in front of us.

Her friends screamed
and ran away.

Kitty wrinkled her nose.
She reached for some paper towels.

"I thought high school parties would be—
I don't know—more
glamorous."

"Sorry to disappoint," I said.

I found myself cornered
In a narrow hallway
by Miranda Price
as I waited
in line for the bathroom.

She towered over me.
She stretched her arm
across the hall
holding a rectangular black clutch
against the wall,
creating a blockade between
me and the bathroom,
me and the party,
me and the rest of humanity.

"I need you
to write my essay,"
Miranda said.

The line dispersed.
Word spread
of a second and third bathroom.
Technically,
I was next in line.

"What essay?" I asked.

Juleah del Rosario

Miranda and I were ranked
#1 and #2
in our class,
and if I was to be completely honest,
she was smarter,
or at least
more tenacious
at being smart
than me.

There was not a single writing assignment
in any of our classes
that Miranda
could not do
in her sleep.

"Cut the crap, Chen.
I know you wrote
Clark Matthews's essay
for his college application.

"He got into Stanford,
and he's dumb as shit."

"You know about that?"

"Everyone knows about that."

Clark Matthews
Last year, a senior
who I sort of knew
from the school newspaper
handed me a sheet of paper.

"I need you to
rip this to shreds,"
he said.
"It's my essay
for my Stanford application."

I half eyed the piece of paper,
and went back to finishing
a newspaper assignment.

He pulled up a chair next to me
and scooted it real close.
"I'm a photographer, not a writer.
I don't know how to make the words say
what I see in my head.
But you do,"
Clark Matthews whispered.

Two days later I found Clark.
"It was shit.
Use this instead."

I handed over two fresh sheets
of typed paper
and walked away.

I hadn't intended
to rewrite his essay,
but when I was editing
his story,
the one he wasn't telling
came to me naturally.

I barely knew Clark.
But in writing his essay
I felt like I saw him,
like the way he saw my articles,

as something more than words.

"I read it,"
Miranda said.
She lowered her arm
and tucked the clutch back underneath.
"It was really good, Nic.
Incredible.

"I'm definitely smarter than you
and my SAT scores are higher than yours,
but
I can't write like that.
I can't make people feel
the way you did
with those words.

"I need you
to write my essay.
I need Stanford."

Maybe I was a little desperate
for attention
that came in the form of compliments.

Maybe I was broken inside,
with a moral compass
that no longer pointed north.

Or maybe I just wanted
to be wanted,
to be heard,
to be seen
by someone.

Anyone.

How drunk
"Miranda, how drunk are you?"
I asked.

"Sober enough to know
what I'm asking."

We both stood
without drinks
in our hands,

outside
a now-empty bathroom.

"Are you really asking me
to write your college essay?"

"A version of it.
A draft.
God, not the final.
That would be
wrong.
I'll rewrite
whatever you give me.
It'll be my words,

my voice
in the end.
But I need you
to start something."

At Meydenbauer High
we were driven by
grade point averages
and rankings
and accolades.

We colored outside the lines,
we broke the mold,
we tore down walls
only when we needed to,
only when it served
our interests.

"What's in it for me?"
I asked.

"Um, I'll pay you?"

"I don't need the money,"
I said.

Gas money, a little extra cash,
college tuition—
it was all provided to me
by a father who thought
that's all I needed
from a father.

"Then what do you want?
A spot on Student Council?
A higher grade in AP Bio?
This handbag?"
She waved the clutch
in front of me.

I wanted a lot
of things.

For senior year
to be easy.

For people not
to hate me.

For Ben.
For love.

"My mom."

The words fell out
as soon as I opened
my mouth.

They floated between us
like two frantic fireflies
unjarred.

The color drained
from Miranda's face.
She bit her lower lip.
"I don't know, Nic,"
she said quietly.

Everyone had a story
about my mother.

She left town.
She didn't want to be found.
No one else wanted
to find her.

But I was still here
in spite of all the gossip.

Trying.

Miranda wanted
to say something,
but I shook my head.

"Money. I'll just take the money."

Laurel LeBrea

Laurel LeBrea, captain of the cheer squad,
could do splits in the air.
She could touch her nose to her kneecap
while her other leg followed obediently
behind,
completing a perfect line.
I kind of hated her for these reasons.

She called.
I silenced the phone.
She left a voice mail.

Why was she leaving
a voice mail?

Nic! It's Laurel.
I heard from Jilly,
who heard from Miranda,
that you are in the business of
writing college admissions essays.
So yeah, I'm definitely interested.
Sign me up.
I'm dying to go to Brown.

Call me!

Packed lunches

"Why does the cafeteria smell like fish
even when it's not Fish Fry Friday?"
I asked.

Kitty nibbled
on a quinoa and kale salad.
"I guess it smells a little."
She kept her head buried
in a textbook
as I sat on the bench
across from her.

"It smells like spoiled milk
and rotten fish."
I emptied the contents
of my lunch bag.

Overripe banana.
Turkey sandwich.
Carrot sticks.

What I wouldn't give
to have my mother back
to pack me lunches
of leftover pork roast,

of pesto and brie,
of grilled vegetable paninis.

To write me notes
on my napkin,
like I'm her little girl,
not the seventeen-year-old
who was supposed to be
grown up enough
to navigate life
without
her mother.

Kitty and I
sat in uncomfortable silence.

She barely raised her eyes
from her book.

Stagnant air
filled my lungs.
"What's going on?"
I asked.

She shrugged and flipped a page.

"What are you studying for?"
I said just to say something.

"Psychology."

"So you can analyze
our friendship," I joked.

"Yeah," Kitty said,
and she flipped another page.

I chewed on my soggy
turkey sandwich in silence

until I opened my mouth
and said something
I probably shouldn't have said.

"What is up with you, Kitty?"

"You didn't text me.
You never called, Nic.

"You took me to a party,
watched me get shit-faced,
and nearly left me there
fawning over some lacrosse boy."

Kitty closed her textbook.
She looked me in the eye.

"Jesus, Nic.
You broke, like, all the rules
of girl code."

Girl Code

1. Don't let your friend get *that* drunk.
   And if she gets *that* drunk,
   you are obligated to
   stay by her side
   the entire rest of the night
   ready to either hold back her hair
   or hold out a wastebasket
   as she pukes up
   her breakfast, lunch, and dinner.

2. Never. Ever let your drunk-ass friend
   sit on the lap of a lacrosse boy.

3. DON'T LEAVE YOUR FRIEND AT A PARTY.

4. Call or text your friend the next morning
   to check in on her.
   Ask her how she feels.
   Be a good friend.
   Show some goddamn sympathy.

So important
"What were you doing on Sunday, Nic,
that was so important
that you couldn't call or text?"

There was the exam
I was studying for in AP Calculus.
Six chapters remained in *Crime and Punishment*.
An essay I formulated for Miranda.

But there was also
the time I whittled away
scrolling through contacts on my phone.
Landing on Ben.
Reading his last text.

Pick you up in ten
And before that
I'm outside the library
And before that
dope
And before that . . .

I read and reread his messages
to get to the one
where he said I was
"special,"

Juleah del Rosario

or the one that made me feel
something
that might have been love,
or the one that would be
the last one
I would need to read
to feel
enough,
today.

"I should have called,"
I said.

A turkey sandwich
sat in a crumbled mess.

Kitty sighed.
"Yeah, you should have."

The new girl
Teetered with a lunch tray
down a row of tables, looking
like a sad, lost Bambi.

"I think we should invite
her
to sit with us,"
Kitty said,
forcing us
to move beyond
the uncomfortable
moment.

Kitty waved.

The new girl
shuffled toward us.

Her hair, her eyes,
her overall demeanor
all looked very—
shiny.

She extended her arm toward me.
Tiny silver bangles, making

Juleah del Rosario

tiny jangling sounds,
slid down.

"I don't think we've been
properly introduced,
but I'm in most of your classes,"
the new girl said.

Her hand remained hanging
midair.

Why would she transfer here
senior year, abandoning
all the friends she had known
her whole life?
Like what Ben
did to us.

What happened *to* her?
Or maybe,
what did *she* do
to cause such a fissure
in her life?

Her bright blue eyes
offered no secrets,

no darkness,
no sadness.

She looked
perfectly fine,
and I felt
a twinge
of jealousy.

"This is Nic."
Kitty nudged.
I forced a polite smile.

What if I had been
the one
to transfer schools,
to abandon everyone
I had ever known
and loved?

But the thought
quickly dissipated.
That wasn't me.

I was still
here.

Your firstborn child
Miranda sat poised
at the edge of a faux-
leather armchair positioned
next to a fireplace,
in what had been deemed
the school's Academic Commons.

Our public school's showcase space
looked like a Starbucks
sans the coffee and baristas,
with sconces illuminating walls
and pendant lights hovering
above cozy tables.

Apparently, taxpayers
were generous.

"Describe, in your own words,
what happened
at last year's Golf Pros
and Tennis Hoes party,"
I said slowly.

We were alone.

"You want me

to tell you
what happened
at a party where
the male population of Meydenbauer
dressed in respectable golf attire,
while the female population
arrived in slutty tennis skirts
and skintight polos?

"And this is for
my college application?"

I nodded.

"I'm applying to Stanford.
Remember?"

I nodded again.
"A sweet, safe, slice-of-life essay
isn't gonna cut it
for an Ivy or any other decent school,"
I said.

"College admissions officers want
to read
something real.

They want to feel
something raw.
In turn, they want us to emote
all over the damn page—
in five hundred words or less."

"You mean—in five hundred words
or fewer,"
Miranda corrected.

"Yeah, I know.
Words are countable objects
so
it
should
be
fewer.

"But I'm not the one
screwing up the grammar.
Read the essay prompt from last year's
Common Application."

Miranda narrowed her eyes.
"I volunteered
in Haiti.

An orphanage
in Haiti.
Why can't you write about that?"

"Hey, I'm just doing my job."
I set down a notebook,
and leaned in close.

"My job
is to get you into college.
Not just any college,
Stanford,
which has an acceptance rate
of 5.1 percent.

"If you want an essay
about a volunteer trip to Haiti,
then write it
yourself.

"But if you want *me*
to write your essay,
then I write it
my way."

Miranda slumped.

She chipped away
at polish on manicured nails.

"What happened at the party
is on YouTube,"
she hissed.
"You can go watch it."

A string of pearls dangled
below her pressed shirt.
She twirled the necklace loosely with a finger.

"I know. I've seen it," I said.
It was ugly, demeaning, and crass.
Crudely shot footage, stalkerish
camera angles,
set to music that made the whole thing seem . . .
addictive.

There were forty thousand views
and counting.

"Whatever it is
that makes you get up every morning
and walk down these halls with your head
held high,

defying the cowardice
of the anonymous creators
of that contemptible video—
that, Miranda,
is college admissions gold."

Miranda sighed.
"I would give my firstborn child
to get into Stanford.

"What do you want to know?"

"I want to know what it felt like
to walk into school
on Monday morning
after the party."

"You're joking, right?
I pay a shrink a hundred and fifty dollars
an hour
to forget that night,
the day after,
the week after,
the month after.
And you want me to tell you
how I felt?

"I take Zoloft to stop feeling."

I nodded.
I knew what it felt like
to be talked about,
to be the source of gossip
that infected
the conversations at school.

Miranda's eyes darted
toward the door,
but no one was there.

"It hurt like hell,"
she said quietly.

"How do you feel
now?"

She shrugged. "About the video?
Or life in general?"

"Both," I said.

"I want to say
I'm over it.

The video,
not life.
But I'm not. It . . ."

She straightened out her skirt.

". . . changed me.
For a week
I was all that anyone talked about.
Then Meydenbauer moved on
to whatever new drama popped up
the next week.

"But for me?
I had to continue to live with the feeling
of everyone staring at me.

"For a month,
every time I saw
a guy staring at his phone
for more than two minutes,
I thought he was watching
my video, watching
me.

"I'm class president.

People stare at me
all the time.

"But this was different."

The bell rang
Miranda glanced up to a spot
where there should have been a clock
but there wasn't.
"Are we done here?"

"Yes. This is perfect,"
I said.

She stood up,
slung a tote over her shoulder,
and disappeared
into the mass of students
who streamed through the hallway.

How many of us
had walked through these halls
and felt
exactly the same
as Miranda?

Austin Schroeder

Was upgraded
to captain of the soccer team.
He rode shotgun in Jordan's SUV.
People started remembering
his name
after Ben left.

Austin Schroeder assumed a place
that Ben emptied.

His curls were tufted.
His smile was soft.
He said "Hi" in the halls.

But he never held the door open
for teachers and freshmen.
He never said
just the right thing
to make a crappy day
better.

Austin Schroeder filled
the empty space,
but he couldn't fill

the void
of Ben.

In Spanish class,
he slid into the seat
next to me.

Señora Torres asked us
to converse with our neighbor.

Austin leaned across the aisle.
"*¿Vas a escribir mi ensayo de la universidad?*"

"*¿Perdón?*" I responded.

"Miranda's Stanford essay,"
he whispered.

"Huh?"

"The smartest girl in school
is asking *you*
to write
her college application essay,"
Austin hissed.

Part of me hesitated,
part of me wanted
to say no,
but instead
I nodded slowly.

Señora Torres walked
up and down the aisles.

"*¿Cuánto cuesta?*" Austin asked.
"*Trescientos dólares,*" I said.

"*¡Ay Dios mío!*"
Austin clutched his chest
like he was an actor
in his own telenovela.

Señora Torres smiled,
charmed by our charade,
then continued walking.

Austin dug into his jacket.
He pulled out a wad of cash
and whispered,
"This should be enough."

"Clase, clase,"
Señora Torres called out
from the front of the room.

"Sí, sí,"
we repeated in unison.

I sighed
and took the money.

"Where are you applying?"
I asked.

Why I write #1
College admissions officers wanted
a comeback story.

They wanted
to cry at the end of an essay.

They wanted
to read about the joy
a student felt
when their life was on
the precipice of change.

They wanted
the underdog,
the scrappy football team
to take down the seasoned champs.

But most of all,
they wanted
to feel.

Most essays paraded
saccharine stories about
good guys or good girls

Juleah del Rosario

with stellar GPAs
and leadership potential.
They were cloying,
they were tedious,
they were stale.

It took brains
to be successful,
but it also took grit
and guts.

Colleges understood this.
I understood this.

When I write
essays, I write
about the emotionally raw
moments,
the lowest points,
the authentic experiences
that change and shape us.

I am more than
writing college essays.
I am telling stories

that we are too afraid to tell,
because to tell them
is to relive them,
and sometimes it hurts

too much.

Donut Day

Laurel LeBrea painted a banner
in sparkly blue and gold
glitter upon glitter upon glitter,
like it was the only logical medium
to express the essence of her creation:

HAPPY DONOR DAY!

Meydenbauer High was a public school,
taxpayer funded, everyone in for free.
Yet our principal envisioned us all
as an elite private school
where *boosters* became *donors*
and AP exams were compulsory.

Football, however,
was no joke.

We were good.
State champions good.
And the *donors* loved us for it.

Ashok groaned.
"I would give

my left arm
for that sign to read HAPPY DONUT DAY
and for a massive pile of donuts
to permanently live
right here."

He made a square with his arms.

"Cake donuts, jelly-filled, Boston cream,
chocolate, chocolate sprinkles,
rainbow sprinkles,
maple bars, bear claws, apple fritters . . ."

"Okay! Donuts over donors.
Best thing ever," I said.

"Yep. My left arm,
is totally worth sacrificing."

"I'll start gnawing
on your arm
if you don't stop talking
about donuts."

I knocked him with my shoulder.

He nudged me back.
We laughed.

Someone cleared their throat.
Our laughter quelled.

A crowd of donors
Stood before us
and stared
like we were an exhibit.

"To our left is Nic Chen,"
our principal said.
"Nic interned last summer
at a biomedical research lab,
where she was on the brink
of curing cancer."

"*Cancer,*"
our principal said again,
with reverence.

The donors looked at me,
awestruck.

In reality,
my internship had consisted of
copying and pasting numbers
into an Excel file
and reformatting researchers' CVs.

I was nowhere close
to curing cancer.

Juleah del Rosario

I had to pass AP Bio first.

"And behind Nic Chen,"
our principal said.

Ashok stepped forward,
but our principal continued,
"Is the Meydenbauer trophy case,
complete with
three consecutive
state championship trophies,
led by star quarterback
Bryant Barnett."

With embarrassing enthusiasm,
the crowd whooped and hollered.

They scooted closer
to get a better view,
but Ashok and I
were in the way,
and we awkwardly
did not move.

So the donors turned
their attention
to Ashok,

eager to hear his tale
of greatness,
in hopes of gaining entrance
to the trophy case.

Our principal furrowed her brow,
as if searching
for something, anything
to say about the guy
wearing rave-green sneakers.

"Ashok," he said, pointing to himself.
"Future AIDS vaccine,
and future husband
of a supermodel, yo!"

A few donors chuckled,
and the alum
famous for marrying a *Real Housewife*
nodded in solidarity.

Our principal's perma-smile
downshifted a gear,
and Ashok and I quickly found an exit
as the crowd inched closer
to the trophy case.

Guys like Bryant

It was like this every fall.
The town of Meydenbauer would obsess
over a guy like Bryant Barnett,
who could rush two hundred and thirty
yards,
pass three hundred and eight,
and score a couple of touchdowns.

We'd watch, huddled under fleece blankets,
sneaking swigs of schnapps,
texting our post-game plans,
throwing down money for a keg.

We'd watch guys like Bryant
on the football field, victorious,
from our mostly white
privilege in the stands.

When Bryant Barnett plays football

He gazes into the stands
between every quarter.
And you know she's there
somewhere,
his girlfriend,
the one he adores,
and loves.

I wonder what it feels like
to be looked for,
to be seen,
to be found.

I wonder what it feels like
to wait
not for the next play,
the next touchdown,
but for the moment
when someone
who loves you
stares into the stands
and sees you

as you are,
authentic and unfiltered.

Juleah del Rosario

A rainbow-sprinkled donut
Sat on top of my desk
at the start of seventh period.

Ashok had powdered sugar
dusted across his chin.
He licked his fingers.

"Got you one,"
he said.

No one had done anything
this nice for me
in a long time,

since Ben.

"Don't get the wrong idea,"
Ashok continued.
"This is a bribe."

I took a bite of the donut.
I still thought
it was pretty darn nice.

"What do you want?"

I asked through a mouthful
of frosted covered awesomeness.

"Study buddies.
You and me, Chen.
AP Bio.
We've got some
Jedi mind-meld going on.
I can feel it.
We should use our powers
for good
grades.

"And I need myself
some good grades."

A smile formed
around the corners of my mouth.

I took another bite and said,
"As long as you bring
the study snacks."

Study buddies
Ashok and I
sat at the dining room table,
beneath the Chihuly sculpture
that functioned
as a light fixture
and hung precariously
from the ceiling.

Muted light shone
through floor-to-ceiling windows
that looked out onto the lake.

It was a luxurious way
to study AP Biology.

Hungry

It roared.
It gnashed its teeth.
It whined like a baby.
It whimpered like a puppy.
And when it grumbled
at a tone where Ashok stopped
studying and looked up,
I finally said,
"I'm hungry."

"There's a bag of food
in your fridge
that my mom sent over,"
he said, and went back to his textbook.

Brain food

The microwave roared to a halt
and beeped persistently.

I opened a container
of what looked like chana masala,
or at least something with chickpeas.

Steam that smelled of coriander
and other unidentifiable spices escaped
in one small puff.

I balanced
the containers of Indian food
on a stack of
plates, napkins, and utensils
and carried them back
to our study space.

"Ashok, if you can continue to supply
your mother's cooking,
you may be my new favorite
study buddy."

Ashok dug into a pile of rice and curry.
"Word."

The Krebs cycle

"I don't understand,"
Ashok said.

"The Krebs cycle," I said.
The page in front of me
was filled with a giant circle
and squiggles,
and arrows.

"I know the Krebs cycle,"
Ashok said.

"What is it? Because
I don't think
I've ever seen
this page before."

Why didn't anyone tell me
how difficult
senior year would be?
How difficult it was to
sit in AP class after AP class,
swallowing facts
by the handful

until you just wanted to vomit
up your entire education.

"It's the process
through which we humans
like other aerobic organisms
generate energy."

I stared at a diagram
of carbon chains.

"It's what allows us
to do anything.
Run a marathon.
Read a book.
Sit here and study,"
Ashok said.

I wanted to do
anything
and everything.

I wanted to ace
AP Bio.

Yet I stared at the page
that continued to make
no sense.

"You got this, girl.
Just watch this YouTube video,"
Ashok said.

I cued up the video
with relief
that today
I wouldn't be
defeated.

Three hundred dollars

"Girl, I don't understand,"
Ashok said again.

"What?"

He pointed out the window.

"You live in this sick house
on the lake with a dock
and a Jet Ski
and a speedboat
and a mechanical lift thingy that keeps
the Jet Ski and the speedboat
out of the water.
Damn that's awesome.

"Yet you charge three hundred dollars
to write college essays
for a bunch of spoiled-ass rich kids.

"You don't even need the money."

"I know," I said.

"Then why the hell do you charge
three hundred bucks?"

"Because I can.
Because it's market value."

"In what market?"

I shrugged.
"We live in Meydenbauer, Ashok."

A modest yacht lumbered
past our dock.

"Not everyone at our school
shits money."

"I know," I said.
But I didn't. Not really.

Everyone I knew had houses
that lined the golf course
or encircled the lake.

Everyone I knew had fathers
who were executives
at Microsoft, Amazon, or
sold their tech start-up
for a couple million.

Everyone I knew had mothers
with platinum credit cards,
Mercedes SUVs,
and addictions to expensive
chardonnays and champagne.

I knew about a lot of things.
I knew how to apply
L'Hospital's rule to evaluate limits
of indeterminate forms.
I knew that Alexander Hamilton
believed that the debt accrued during
the Revolutionary War was the price
we had to pay for liberty and freedom.
I knew the difference
between an epistrophe and an anastrophe.

I knew what it felt like
to be enveloped
by expectations.

What I didn't know

"Do you know
our star quarterback?"
Ashok asked.

"Of course. Bryant Barnett,"
I said.

"Do you know
his stats?"

"Of course,
All-American,
three state championships,
forty-two touchdown passes
just last season."

"Do you know
why he plays for Meydenbauer?"

"Uh, because he's good."

"But do you know
who cleans the men's locker room?"

"No. Why would I?
What's your point,

Ashok?"

"How do you think
a kid like Bryant Barnett
ended up in a place like Meydenbauer?"

"The same way the rest of us got here—
our parents,"
I said.

"You think Bryant's parents live
in a house like this?
Work in a place like Microsoft?"

"I don't know,
maybe,"
I said.

"You don't know shit."

Keyword searching
Staff
Directory
Meydenbauer High

"So you're saying
Bryant Barnett's father
is a janitor at Meydenbauer?"
I asked.

Ashok looked up from his textbook.
"Can you at least
read a draft of my boy Bryant's essay?
As a favor?"

"Sure," I said.
"Like you said,
I don't need the money."

I did what my father told me
To make him proud,
to make him love me.

I excelled in math and science.
I went to Chinese school
for eight years,
every morning.

I respected my elders
when they came to visit.
I ate everything off my plate.

Yet it was never enough
for him to stop working
so late.

Mom didn't help
the situation either.

I did what they told me,
and yet

we lived in a household
where my parents
avoided coexisting with each other,

where they were clearly
the worst roommates,
where their only daughter
served as some sort of Switzerland.

I should have asked
"Do you even love each other?"
to my parents
at some point.

But I knew the answer.
My parents did not marry for love.

Mom saw my father at a party.
She said he was cute
She said he had social cache
and a reputation,
whatever that means
at MIT.

My father,
from China,
here on an F1 visa,
was focused,
determined,
and fascinated

with beautiful,
blond,
talkative
American girls
like my mother.

Mom got pregnant.
Dad insisted on marriage,
partially to defy his family
who expected him to return
after graduation
and partially because,
as a good Chinese man,
he felt obligated
to take on the duties
of fatherhood.

Everything Dad had grown to understand
about the American dream—
the good job,
the stable family,
the fancy cars—
crumbled in on him
the day Mom left.

Dad walked around untethered
for months.
He stayed at the office
most nights.
He went in on weekends.
Until one day
he, too,

up and left,
just like Mom.

But at least he gave me his flight info
and a phone number
while he was away in China.

He trusted that I could take care of myself,
not because I had earned it,
but because he didn't know any better.

He didn't know me.

I threw a house party
Two years ago
while Dad was in China
and Mom was
God knows where.

I invited everyone I knew
and then some.

I wanted a house filled
with something
other than
loneliness.

Strangers filled empty spaces,
squeezing by,
finding friends
and a beer.

The boy
who sat next to me in Spanish,
who smelled like cut grass,

who gave me
the good cheese and the good crackers
out of his Lunchable
in third grade,

stood on the other end
of the kitchen.

Ben and I were friends
in first grade.

He told me jokes.
He let me drive his Power Wheels
up and down the block.

But our friendship
had faded as

Ben, Jordan, and I
became Ben and Jordan

and I
was left to find

friends who wore makeup,
friends who wanted boyfriends,
friends who were like
Audrey and Jenny and Jilly.

We had a past together,
but tonight
something inside me hinted

that maybe we had a future.

Maybe
was what his sly smile said
from across the kitchen.

I didn't need alcohol to approach Ben,
but it certainly helped.
"Hola, amigo," I said.

Ben leaned against the counter.
Our bare arms touched.
He drank a Keystone Light
slowly,
like it was a can full of something
far more satiating.

He tipped it back.

I knocked his shoulder.
"Empty?"

He shrugged.

But the way his mouth stretched
across his face,

the way his charm stretched
across our conversation,

made the fuzzy boundaries
of my skin
grow boundless.

I should have known
a boy's shrug
meant apathy,
not answers.

But I wanted so badly to be
all his answers.

One of the twins jostled me.
Jenny or maybe Audrey.
I couldn't tell tonight.

Ben reached out
and pulled me out of the way,
pulled me closer
to him,

and closer to
the opposite

of loneliness.

The moment passed,
and he dropped his arm,
but I wanted
more than anything
for that arm to linger
longer
around my shoulder.

I wanted to feel it
again.

"My dad has better stuff
to drink. You want?"
I said.

He nodded,
his tousled brown hair messy
in the just-rolled-out-of-bed
kind of way.

"Follow me."
I pushed our way through the crowd
to the end of an empty hall.

We entered the study

with a fireplace, a leather couch,
and sconces casting solitary shadows.

A cabinet sat behind an oak desk,
which I unlocked with a key.
"Whiskey, bourbon, or scotch?"
I said.

Ben stood behind me.
He laid his palm lightly on my shoulder
as if to crane his head around for a better
view.
I felt his warm breath on my neck.
I turned around and looked up.

The room spun
and I was drunk
on love
and alcohol.

I ran my fingers along the side of his body.
He squirmed
and smirked
and grabbed my hand in his.
He pulled me closer.
Our lips met.

It felt drunken
at first,
then real.

He tugged at the zipper on my dress,
fumbled with the clasps on my bra.
I unlocked my lips and stepped away.

"Not here."
I rehooked my bra
and zipped up my dress.

"Have you ever had
a five-thousand-dollar bottle
of whiskey?" I asked.

Ben's eyes widened,
his lips now glossy
like mine.

I poured us both
a glass of Glenrothes 1970
single-malt whiskey.
I handed him a crystal tumbler.
We clinked glasses and sipped
the caramel-colored alcohol.

We nosed the complexity of the drink.
I couldn't tell whether it smelled
oaky, or citrusy, or sweet, or acrid.
"It's a shame I'm too drunk
to appreciate this," I said.
Ben nodded and took another sip.

"Let's get out of here," I said.
I wove my hand in his
and led him back through
the mass of bodies
sweating alcohol and cheap cologne.

We wound our way
to the other side
of the house,
ending at a door
that led upstairs
to my bedroom.

At the top of the stairs
we found solace
in a moonlit room
nestled among the pines.

I untangled my hand from his
and fell on top of my bed.

I closed my eyes
and listened to the rain
that drummed against the windows.

Ben fell on top of me.
His mouth tasted like
five-thousand-dollar whiskey
and his cotton shirt smelled
of cheap beer.

He tugged at my zipper
and fumbled with my bra.
This time I didn't stop him.

That song Mom would always play said
you can't always get what you want,
but that night
I had exactly what I wanted.
I had Ben,

and that was enough.

On our first real date
Ben took me to a movie.
One with superheroes
and lots of CGI effects.

Before the house lights went down
and we settled deeper into the faux-leather
recliners,
before we fixed our eyes on the twenty-by-
fifty screen
and fell out of consciousness with the world
around us—our unanswered texts,
the piles of homework that lay at home—

Ben's eyes found mine
in the dim light,
and for a moment

I thought
he saw me
for who I was—
a girl, anxious
and possibly in love.

Bryant Barnett
The decorated quarterback
of our venerated football team,
motioned to an empty seat.

"Do you mind?" Bryant Barnett asked.
I shook my head.

He swung his enormous quads
over the bench and sat down.
"Ashok said you could help me."
His eyes darted to the girls next to us,
preoccupied with their phones.
"But I can't . . ."

". . . pay. I know,"
I said softly.
Bryant grimaced.

Three hundred dollars was less than
a new iPhone and slightly more than
a new pair of skinny jeans from Nordstrom.

But three hundred dollars
was more than a week's worth of pay
from a part-time job
at the deli counter at Safeway.

Was I so wrong
to charge
what the market
would bear?

"I'm the oldest.
I'm the first to have a shot,"
Bryant continued.
"College means everything to me.

"I'll go to Oregon.
I'll play football if I have to.

"But Elbridge College—
if I can get in,
get a full-ride
without being an athlete—
that would be
life-changing.

"It's a long shot, I know.
But, man, it would be
an achievement."

An achievement
"What about winning three state
championships?
Hoisting a trophy above your head?
Smiling into all those flashing bulbs?
Getting caught in a confetti shower?

"Being wanted by all the top recruiters?
Pursuing a Heisman?"
I asked.

"Winning a Heisman
isn't winning
life, Nic.

"And football isn't
the game I need to play
for my future,"
Bryant said.

When Bryant Barnett wore
A #BlackLivesMatter shirt
after another police shooting last fall,
it made the school
uncomfortable,

as if to remind us
that he is more than
a football star,
more than a golden boy,
more than a pawn
in our town's obsession
with greatness,

as if to remind us
that Bryant Barnett
is black.

We forget that race exists—
Because it's so much easier
to pretend
it's not there.

It's so much easier
to try to blend in
like neutral beige foundation
soaked into skin.

But it's there
in line at the grocery store
when the White cashier
wrinkles her nose
at the bottle of fish sauce
and can of bean curds
Xiaoling has found
in the *Asian* aisle at
Whole Foods.

It's there on the playground
at the downtown park
when someone else's mother
grabs me by the arm
and asks,
"Who do you
belong to?"

Juleah del Rosario

It's there in the East parking lot
after school as some White guys
blast Kanye
from a thousand-dollar stereo,
as if his words
speak their truth.

It's there when you see
a Toyota Camry
driving down Main Street
driven by a black man
being tailed
by an officer.

But the stoplight turns green
and we keep on driving,
distancing
ourselves
from what makes us
uncomfortable.

To own

"Don't do what you do for everyone else,"
Bryant said.
"Just read it. Tell me
if it sucks.

"This one's mine
to own.
Okay?"

I nodded. "Of course."

Bryant Barnett slid a single sheet
across the table.

I took the essay in hand.
I fell into the weight of the words
he stood to own.

I began to read.

Elbridge College Application

Written by Bryant Barnett

Elbridge College offers ample opportunity for students to explore activities in the arts, athletics, sciences, social life, and in the community. In 500 words or fewer, tell us who you will be and what you may do as a student at Elbridge College.

I have a powerhouse arm and countless records in yards rushing. I've taken Meydenbauer High to the state championships three out of four years of high school. I train seven days a week, lifting in the mornings, drills and scrimmages in the afternoon, to prep for the Friday-night game.

To play football here in Meydenbauer, to be coached by the best, to be on the state's most established team requires my dad to work three jobs and my mom to work weekends. We live in the cheapest apartment complex there is within the school district boundaries. My little brother is the only Black kid in his fifth-grade class. My family has sacrificed a lot to live in Meydenbauer, to have me play here, at this high school.

You have the worst football team in the nation. Division III and you have won only one game in five years. But I want to attend Elbridge because I want to be more than a football player. In America, this is not what young black men are supposed to do. We are supposed to go to college to be student-athletes, athletes first.

Meydenbauer has a great football program, but it is also one of the best public schools in the country. I came here as an athlete, but I'm leaving here as a student. Mary Shelley's *Frankenstein* mesmerized me. The law of momentum conservation was handy on and off the field. While I found AP US History to be all too whitewashed, I thoroughly appreciated my world history teacher's syllabus on the non-"Western" world.

I want to go to Elbridge, not because you have a terrible team, but because your football players are people. Last year's captain is now in the Peace Corps. Your running back took a semester off during football season to intern for the White House. Every Monday night one of your linebackers cooks a locally sourced, vegan meal for the entire team.

Why am I, as a black man, limited to being an athlete in order to go to college? Why do I have to rely on a full ride provided by an athletic scholarship in order to attend?

At Elbridge College, I want to be more than an athlete, more than a black man who has a great arm. At Elbridge College, I want to be a whole person.

Half a life
I couldn't shake
the last line
from Bryant Barnett's essay.
What did it mean to be
a whole person?

For most of high school,
I felt like I had been living
half a life.

Then,
for the brief eight months
I was with Ben,
there was
a new sense of roundness,
like I was a balloon
suddenly inflated.

Thoughts of Ben clung to me

Everything still reminded me of Ben.
Walking down the halls.
Seeing a familiar shadow
dart into a classroom.
Driving across the lake.
Eating a sandwich.

Thoughts of Ben were like humidity,
just there, on my skin,
there, when I breathed.

Last spring
I held his hand as we drove
across the lake
and inched through traffic
along I-90 and up I-5.

I let go as we wound our way
through the leafy streets
until we arrived at the end of the road,
at the edge of the city limits.

We stopped at a shack
outside a park
and ordered

pork sandwiches.

I took a bite. "OMFG."

Sauce and grease and everything amazing
dribbled down my face.
Ben laughed and reached over
and brushed my face
with a paper napkin.

I wanted to kiss him.
I hesitated.
I had food in my mouth.

But then he leaned over
and licked my cheek
like I was a Popsicle.

I burst out laughing.
"You're such a weirdo," I said.

He shrugged
like it was no big deal.

And we both went back
to eating our sandwiches,

the best sandwiches ever.

I had a lot of bests with Ben,

and now I wasn't sure
where all those bests
had gone.

At the Starbucks

On Northeast 8th
I waited
for coffee.

Marco handed me
a double tall cappuccino,
extra foam.
He wore thick-rimmed glasses
that fogged
a little
every time he frothed
the milk.

"Nicola, you look radiant,"
he said.

Marco believed
everyone's name
should sound
European.

"I love that scarf.
Is it Pucci?"
he asked.

Before my mother
gallivanted away,
she dumped an armload
of clothes, scarves,
and shoes that were one size
too big
on my bedroom floor.

She called herself
a fashionista,
but her therapist called her
a shopping addict.

I brushed the silk scarf
away from my neck.
There was a time
it was a staple
to the outfits
I'd wear
when out
with Ben.

I thought it made me
look sophisticated,
like somebody's
girlfriend,

like a girl
who was supposed to be
with a boy
like Ben.

I checked the tag
sewn into a corner.
"Hermès," I said.

Marco's eyes widened.
"Tell me a French lover
gave that to you
while holidaying in Nice."

I smiled politely and shrugged.
"Sorry. It's from my mother.
Maybe her story is better?"

I wondered if it was.
I wondered if she was off
creating better stories,
in the South of France or Spain
or Argentina
or Morocco.

I wondered, briefly,
why she hadn't called.

I wondered, even more briefly,
if she had forgotten
all about me,
here in Meydenbauer,
where I still live,
in the same home
she left.

"I can't create
In words,"
Marco said
after school last week.

So he paid me
to write
his art school essay,

and last night
I wrote
pieces of it.

I fell into his shoes.
I wandered around
in his world
until the words came out
to greet me.

The essay prompt
was something about
obsession.

I didn't really know
anything about
Marco's obsession.

But I imagined
what his obsession might be,
because wasn't there only one thing
we were truly ever obsessed with?

So I wrote,
and I wrote,
and I wrote, about
love.

A Draft of Marco's Essay

Art can be an endeavor in obsession with sometimes profound or detrimental outcomes. Describe a time when you found yourself obsessed with an idea, concept, or thing. How has this experience influenced your understanding of yourself as an artist?

Portrait of Shane

I used to think I was obsessed with lots of things. A single melody from an up-and-coming songstress. A pleated jacket from New York Fashion Week. The new fro-yo shop that opened up next door to work. I had no idea what it meant to be obsessed until I met Shane. Or, more correctly, I had no idea what it meant to be obsessed until I met Shane, dated Shane, and then lost Shane when he left to join the Peace Corps, somewhere I couldn't even visit on weekends.

I was smitten. I was in love. I devoured the time we spent together. He said words to me that I've never known any other human to say. He touched me with fingers that were both bitter and sweet. He listened to me. He nodded along with all the outlandish ideas I proposed. He hugged me hard. He kissed me harder. For one entire summer, he was all mine.

Then he took it away. He left to listen, to hug, to say things to other people more deserving in this world. Now I am obsessed.

I refresh his page every other minute. I send him cat memes and notes with emoticons. I am not one who emotes in ASCII. I am not a lover of cats. I DO NOT KNOW WHY I SEND HIM THESE THINGS. I'm obsessed with checking my messages. When he replies, I feel like he sent me a cookie, like I ate a cookie, and then I want another. So I search for more cat memes, more emoticons to express how I feel, in order to receive another message, to eat more cookies. I am the freaking Cookie Monster.

As an artist, I'm not sure my obsession does me any good. Under the influence of love, I make bad art. I collage his face. I acrylic his body. I photograph his every angle in every light. The gaudiness in this world is a product of obsessive love like mine.

There are very few works that have gotten love right.

Félix González-Torres's *Untitled (Portrait of Ross in L.A.)*, a 175-pound pile of candy, depleted over time to represent the ideal weight of his dying lover. Who could possibly create a work as poignant and devoted as that? I have a lot to learn.

I love the process of creating art. The hours spent meticulously creating something, planning, experimenting, and feeling the work. The love that I have for the process is the type of love I want with someone else, a slow love, not one born of obsession.

Ben used to bring me
Double tall
soy vanilla lattes
every morning.

I used to bring him
an Egg McMuffin
sandwich.

"You guys are, like,
so mature,"
Jilly would exclaim.

"You *never* buy me coffee,"
Jenny would whine at Jordan.

"That's because you're not
my girlfriend,"
Jordan would respond.

"That's not what everyone else
thinks."
Jenny would smirk.

"Wanna walk me to class?"
Ben would ask,
and I'd nod gleefully back.

"You guys are sooo cute,"
Jilly would say,

and Ben and I would walk away
hand in hand
down the hall.

"Do I have to bring you
a latte tomorrow?"
Ben would whisper.

"I guess not,"
I would say.
"But I'll still bring you
an Egg McMuffin."

"You don't have to."

"But I want to."

"But you don't have to,"
Ben would say.

But the next morning
Ben would hand me
a double tall soy vanilla latte,

and I'd hand over
an Egg McMuffin.

Jilly would swoon
and Jenny would pout,

and Ben and I
would walk
hand in hand
down the hallway
and off to class,
again,

neither of us
considering
what we actually
needed.

What does a pumpkin spice latte taste like?
I slipped into a gray upholstered armchair
and waited for Laurel LeBrea.

"OMG, Nic.
I have some
uh-mazing ideas
for my college essay,"
she said over voice mail
this morning.

When Laurel moved to Meydenbauer
from Southern California
in sixth grade,
I thought she was
the oddest girl I had ever met.
I was pretty sure
she thought
the same of me.

"My daddy's an entertainment lawyer.
What does your daddy do?"
was the first thing she ever said to me,
and I stared at her
and her pink bow
and couldn't comprehend
how Laurel LeBrea's father

could be an entertainment lawyer
in a city with no entertainment.

Laurel strolled into Starbucks
with her sleek blond hair
curled perfectly
around her face.

She tucked her oversize sunglasses
into her purse
and glanced around.

She waved at me
with her fingers,
then headed to the barista.
I sipped the now lukewarm
cappuccino.

Laurel returned with a venti drink.
She took a small sip and squealed.
"Oh my God.
I love pumpkin spice lattes.
It tastes like
a million hugs."

If only
drinking a pumpkin spice latte

was like
a million hugs,
then maybe
everything would be
okay.

But what good
are a million hugs,
when you really only
want one?

Ben's hugs
Were epic.

I loved snuggling deep
against his ratty old T-shirt
that smelled like cut grass and laundry soap.
I loved being enveloped in his arms.

It was like we fit together,
perfectly,
in our hugs.
A yin and a yang.

I used to think
that meant something,
us fitting together
perfectly,
but it wasn't a sign
of anything.

"I think I love you," Ben once said,
while we were interlocked together
like puzzle pieces.

I kissed his forehead

and squeezed him tighter, and
all I could think was
But do you know me?

Smiling makes us happy
In front of us sat Laurel's iPad,
filled with photos of Laurel
at varying stages of life.

Smiling with pigtails at summer camp.
Smiling as a sixth grader in front of her
house.
Smiling as she's being tossed in the air,
her arms outstretched,
her body in a perfect V.

She pointed to a photo of little Laurel
riding a horse.
"I used to be a horse girl, but
it wasn't my scene.
Horse girls are sullen.
I switched to cheer.
Cheer makes people happy.
What about that idea?"

"No,"
I said.

"This is me
at last year's state championship."

She pointed to a photo
of her spiraling through the air.
"What about an essay on
my rise to cheer captain?"

"No," I said
again.

"Do you have any photos
where you're not so—
smiley?"

"I always smile in photos."

I pointed to
the most boring photo on the screen,
the one of Laurel in front of her house.
"Tell me about this one."

"I don't know why
I included that photo.
I don't like it.
I forced that smile.
But I still look cute,
right?"

I touched the screen
to expand the image.
Her smile *was* different.
All mouth and no eyes.
"What's going on here?"

She sighed and fell back into the chair.
"I had just moved to Meydenbauer.
I was supposed to wear
leopard-print flats,
my favorite pair of Sevens,
and a bright pink sweatshirt
that said BE BRAVE,
with a heart around it.
Mom had picked it out for me.

"It was supposed to be
my first-day-in-a-new-school outfit.
I was going to make
all sorts of friends
while wearing it.

"Mom folded it up
and put it on the top of my suitcase.
But when I opened my suitcase

in Meydenbauer,
it wasn't there.
Nor was my mom.
So I cried."

Laurel's story continued,
but I was stuck in the moment
when her mother
was gone.

I knew of the panic
that settles in
on those initial days
without a mother.

"Where is she?"
I said.
The words came out,
interrupting.

Laurel flinched.
"California.
My parents split.
Mom was sad.
Dad wasn't.
It was all very—confusing."

She paused,
and smiled widely
again.

"She's good now.
Very centered.
We talk every day.
I mean, looking back,
she was kind of
not that stable.
I'd always try to
cheer her up.

"It's another reason
I joined cheer.
To actually cheer
people up."

Would I ever get to that place
with my mom?
When I would be able to say
she's good,
centered?
That we talk every day?
Maybe it would happen—
if she ever returned.

Laurel looked back at the photo.
"Dad promised
he'd send her a photo
so that she knew I was
happy.

"I wanted to look happy for her.
That's why I'm smiling."

"Your mom, Laurel.
That's the essay I'll write."

"But it's so depressing,
and totally not fun."
Laurel slumped.

"But it's real."

Laurel nodded hesitantly,
holding a brave smile.

Where's Mom?
I had to say it to myself,
in the days after she
left.

I looked in every closet.
I opened every door.
I checked the garage twice
for missing modes of transportation.

For three straight days,
I repeated,
twice a day,
like brushing my teeth,
like it was normal,
like it was my chore
to find my mom.

"Seriously, where are you, Mom?"
I asked.
But no one was around
to answer my question.

A Draft of Laurel LeBrea's Essay

We have often heard from alumni that their closest friend in college, for the rest of their lives, is the person they roomed with during their first year at Brown. Part of the closeness of freshman-year roommates is the bond that is formed over the mutual process of navigating the rules of dorm life together. Write a letter to your future roommate. What should they know about you? What rules do you wish to establish? What are your fears about roommates, dorm life, or college?

Dear future roomie,

You can borrow my clothes. I have always wanted to say that, but I'm an only child, so there never has been a sister to share clothes with. What's your size? What's your style aesthetic? You can borrow my frilly tops to wear to parties, the sparkly earrings to wear to class, or the aviators to wear while chillin' on the quad. You can borrow almost anything—I swear—except the sweatshirt in my closet that is probably too small for the both of us anyway. It's the tiny gray one, with a big heart and letters in cursive that say BE BRAVE. The tags are still on.

I carry it with me because it reminds me of my mom and reminds me of all the times I'm brave without her. I was supposed to wear this on my first day of school in sixth grade, when I moved to Meydenbauer. But it somehow never got packed in the boxes or in my suitcase when we left my mom in California and my dad and I moved to Washington State. I was supposed to pose in a picture in front of our new house to show my mom what a brave and happy daughter she had raised, that I wasn't devastated that we'd left her behind, that only two-thirds of our family got to embark on this shiny new adventure.

What I didn't know is that my mom went to rehab shortly thereafter. She had an unhealthy relationship with alcohol. She is an alcoholic, which leads me to my biggest fear in college—drinking. I go to parties all the time. I love dancing. I love hanging out with my friends. I'm a big fan of standing by the chip bowl and crushing some salsa and guac. But I don't drink. I haven't drank.

I'm worried about the pressure to drink in college, the friends I may not make because of it. I'm worried you will think that I'm boring and no fun. But most of all, I'm worried that I will drink someday and love it in the way that my mom loved it, in the way that one glass of wine was never enough.

I know that's a lot to take in, future roomie, but there are no words to express how excited I am to share with you the triumphs and tears that comprise the freshman-year experience.

Love always,
Laurel

Our AP English teacher

Stood before us
in an A-line skirt
and four-inch heels.
Her hair was pulled back in a chignon,
and not a strand was out of place.
She held a dog-eared copy of Dostoyevsky's
greatest work
and asked,
"What are the crimes
in *Crime and Punishment?*"

"Murder!" someone shouted.
A few people snickered.

Our teacher rolled her eyes.
"That answer
will not get you
into Harvard."
She paused
and looked at all of us.

"That's what you want,
isn't it?"

Silence slumped over us.
Of course it's what we wanted.

It's why we sacrificed
our weekends,
our sleep,
our sanity.

"Dig deeper, people."
Pages flipped fervently.
Our teacher paced
up and down the aisles.

She smelled like intimidation,
if that's even possible.

I raised my hand
with confidence
and said,
"It depends,"
before I was even
called on.

Faces turned in my direction,
like they always do,
and someone
from the back of the room
coughed "*Slut.*"

Our teacher raised her finger.

"No one in this class
gets a letter of recommendation
if you all keep this up,"
she yelled.

Miranda shot a look
to the boys
in the back row.

I rolled my eyes
and continued.
"Raskolnikov rationalizes
the murder
so much so
that he believes
what he committed
was not a crime at all.
So it depends
on who
is defining *crime*,"
I said.

I understood what Dostoyevsky
was trying to say.

When we saw something
as rational,

how could it possibly
be wrong?

But what I didn't say
is that Dostoyevsky also knew
that we were human,

and sometimes we were meant
to feel
guilt.

There were no secrets
At Meydenbauer.
Jilly slept with a college guy.
A sophomore totaled his Audi S4.
I was in the business
of writing other people's
college application essays
for money.

I was a somebody again.
A somebody who mattered
to the fabric of the school,
whom people needed,
depended on,
who was deemed worthy enough
by the masses
who pushed their way through the halls
during passing period.

Then I saw Jordan.
He saw me.
And like in a movie,
everything around us
cycled by in a blur,
but the air between us
stood still.

This time he didn't smirk.
He stared at me,
eyes unreadable,
until our line of sight no longer
connected.

The stillness ended.
I remained alone, jostled
in every direction by the masses
that pushed their way through the hall
during passing period.

But the image of Jordan's eyes hung
in front of me
like a mirage.

They were gray.
I had always known
they were gray.

When we were together
I didn't know the color
of Ben's eyes.

I could see him looking
at me, staring and blinking
and opening
his eyes
wide
like he was paying attention.

He closed his eyes,
then opened them
dramatically wider, signaling,
I'm listening,
and I saw his eyes
do this, so I started
talking, blathering,
but I stopped
because I asked
a question
and I waited for a response
that I never got,
because he wasn't listening
and I didn't know
the color
of Ben's eyes.

Tell me I'm pretty #1

"Tell me I'm pretty, Ben."

"You know you're pretty, Nic."

"But I'm your girlfriend.
You're supposed to say
these things
to me," I said.

He kissed my forehead
and said
nothing.

A million versions of me
Walked the halls
of Meydenbauer.

There were the versions of me
that were easy to see:
the tennis champ me,
the newspaper me,
the perfect SAT me,

the driven me,
the studious me.

There were the versions of me
that were not so easy to see:
the long hours of me
who sat by a window with a textbook,
struggling
to push away
the longing sighs for her mother.

The anxious me
who held her boyfriend's hand tight
and her emotions tighter.

The lonely me
who could be surrounded by

people at a party
and still feel disconnected
from the whole world.

I sat in an unused corner
Of the cafeteria
knocking out
a calculus problem set
because Kitty was nowhere
to be found,
and Ashok was somewhere
off-campus.

But in the back of my mind,
past the derivatives and integrals,
I drifted over thoughts of Ben.

There was a barbecue
at his house
last May.

Clumps of self-absorbed people
scattered about the yard
like the patches of grass
that survived
the frost and the winter
still intact,
still green.

I stood to the side of Ben,
watching the party

Juleah del Rosario

hold itself off
from dying.

I was tired, cranky, and sober.

I tried to nuzzle my head into his shoulder.
The muscles around his back grew tight.
He stiffened.
I drew away.
He flashed
an empty smile.

There was a sliver of space
between us,
where our skin no longer touched,
a void that I felt
drain of softness.

His glassy eyes gazed
through my sadness,
my fear,
the anxiety
that shivered on my skin.

I saw an empty smile
that looked at me and said,
I don't know who you are.

"Grab a beer for me, babe?"
he whispered.

I wanted Ben to notice
that my eyes were heavy,
that my smile had faded.

I wanted to curl up
on a couch next to him.

I didn't want
to be here,
pretending.

"Get your own fucking beer,"
I said.

Ben pouted

as loneliness crept back
into the cracks
inside me.

When every exam becomes a midterm
We were well past the middle of the term
and so it didn't make sense
why every exam administered in every class
was labeled "midterm."

We had three midterms in AP Bio,
four in AP Government,
and I swear there was a midterm
every other week
in AP Calculus.

I almost looked forward to finals
for the sake of veracity,
when a final meant
a final,
a last,
a determination
of something
like our future.

Edna St. Vincent Millay

The new girl read to us
a poem
by Edna St. Vincent Millay
in a voice that lulled the classroom
and made our teacher smile.

"Is this poem supposed to teach us
not to sleep around,
lest we end up old and alone?"
someone conjectured.

I heard the words of lips and lovers,
of a lonely tree
and birds that vanish.

"I think it's about the ephemeral
nature of love.
It won't be around forever,"
someone else said.

"It's about loneliness,"
Jordan responded.

"Care to expand?"

our teacher asked.

He shook his head.
"It's obvious."

Which tree is the most lonely?
The one with
or without
birds?

I saw the loneliness
as clearly as Jordan.

I saw my mother.

What lovers has she forgotten?
Which feelings have stirred a quiet pain?

What ghosts visit her nightly
and tap on her window
like rain?

How could she forget
the love that life brought?

How could she
leave behind
me?

I'm not fine, Mom
I felt like you left
and the whole house emptied.

I felt like you left
and my whole heart emptied.

I felt like you left
and I wasn't your daughter—because you left
me.

You emptied me, Mom.
I didn't know you could.
I didn't see it before—how much

I am still
your daughter.

If I were to pinpoint where it all went wrong
It was polishing off a bottle of Jameson
with Jordan
last summer,
at his party.

Or maybe lingering too long in the kitchen
with Jordan
and not Ben.

Or maybe it was
Jordan's question
that wriggled under my skin
and wouldn't let me go.

"Why the sad smile, Nic?"

If Ben were to describe me
He would have said I was the smartest
student at Meydenbauer,
at least I hope.

Or maybe he'd describe me as
pretty and cute,
like rainbows and puppy dogs,
lake views and llamas.

Or maybe he'd say
she's the girl inside
with the long brown hair
wearing a T-shirt and jeans,
talking to Jordan.

But if Ben were to see me
Would he see the way
I watched him,
as we all did,

nearly land in a fire pit
in a failed attempt
to ride a skateboard
over an asinine jump?

Would he see the way
I gulped down
too much Jameson
and not enough Coke?

Would he see the way
I was drunk and crying
and never
ask me why,

or did he see the way
I deflated
over time

like tires
on an old bicycle?

"Where are your parents?"
I asked as we watched someone
we both didn't know
do a keg stand
in Jordan's kitchen.

Jordan tipped his empty
cup, then topped off
both of our drinks.

"Avoiding each other's
existence."

"So they're gone for the weekend?"

"They're just gone."

"Like my mom?"

"No. Like my parents,"
he said.

We both said nothing,
and watched
the kid at the keg
wipe away beer that drenched
his face.

"Wanna do a keg stand?"
Jordan asked.

"Fuck no," I said.

"Well, talking about our parents
is a buzzkill,"
he said,
and downed his drink.

In the kitchen
Jordan and I swapped
embarrassing stories.
We laughed
at jokes I don't remember.

We bantered.
We listened,
we felt better,
we cared.

We lightly touched each other
on the arm,
on the face, and then,
somehow,
we ended up
upstairs, no longer

in the kitchen.

Tell me I'm pretty #2

"Tell me I'm pretty, Jordan."

"You don't want
to be pretty, Nic."

"Why not?"

"Pretty is conventional.
It's dull perfection.
It's attractiveness without
being truly beautiful."

"Then what am I, Jordan?"

He shook his head and sighed.

"The way you fidget,
the way you roll your eyes,
the way you say very little
and everything
all at once,

you're beautiful, Nic,
but you're not perfect."

Tires screeching #1

Through the open second-story window
I heard Ben's truck
sputter and then start.
I heard him rev his engine
while still in park,
to keep it from

dying.

I ran to the window
naked

just in time to see
Ben—my ride,
my boyfriend—

drive away,

at a speed that
left the sound
of tires screeching around a corner
reverberating in my ears
long after he

left.

I turned around and screamed
"What the fuck, Jordan?
Why did you make me do it?"

"I didn't fucking make you do
anything."

Jordan sat up.
He rifled around under the covers.
He threw a bra, underwear, a T-shirt
that wasn't even mine

at me.

He slid out of bed and picked up a pair of
boxers
off the floor,
then walked,
disheveled,
into the adjacent bathroom.

He shut the door.
The lock clicked in place.

I fished around the floor,
for the rest of my clothes,
and haphazardly tugged on

a T-shirt and jeans
and jammed my feet
into a pair of laced-up sneakers.

I opened Jordan's bedroom door
and left it wide open.

Downstairs,
in the kitchen,
half-empty Solo cups
of whiskey and Coke
littered the countertops.
On the table,
lay an unfinished game
of beer pong.

Outside,
stragglers smoked
cigarettes and weed.

I slipped out the front door
unnoticed.

My ride

I dialed Kitty's number.
I knew she'd be home.
She had parents who were
responsible—

who cared where she was
at one in the morning.

My dad, stepmother, and stepbrother
were in China for two weeks,
and my mom—

who knows?

There was no one holding me accountable
for my actions
at this hour.

She answered on the fourth ring.
"Nic?"

"Can you pick me up?"

Kitty could have told me
to walk the three miles home
like we've done before.

"Uh, sure," she said groggily.
"I've got to put on some clothes.
Find my car keys.
Tell my parents."

The air was warm and sticky.
It felt better
than being tangled under the sheets
with Jordan.

"Your parents?"

"I can't just drive off with the car
in the middle of the night.
They'll understand.
We want you to be safe."

They all cared,
and it almost felt
like too much.

"Is everything okay?" Kitty asked.
I wanted to say no.

"My ride left," I said.

Left.

"Ben?"
I didn't answer.

"Tell me where you are."
I looked at the street sign.

I'm on the corner of forever,
I didn't say.

I said something else,
then hung up.

The sky began to rumble.
It lit up, briefly,
before going black again.

In Meydenbauer
thunderstorms were rare.
I couldn't remember that last time I'd seen
one.
I was probably too young
or too scared.

I sat on someone's manicured front lawn,
waiting for Kitty,
waiting for the summer storm to roll through.

I knew that Ben knew.
It didn't really matter how.

He just did,
and he drove away,

tires screeching around a corner.

The next afternoon
I found myself
back upstairs
in his room.

I found Jordan shirtless
in his bed, holding
a controller for his Xbox, shooting
at humans, orcs, and elves.

"Are we supposed to be together?"

Jordan barely glanced over from the screen,
but when he did,
I caught a glimpse in his eyes.
Something flickered like a faulty bulb,
and then it was gone.

In its place
a vacant expression.

"I doubt it,"
Jordan said.

Last night, here in his room,
strings of sadness had knotted us together.

We didn't solve anything.
We didn't untangle
our tangled parts,
but the closeness,
the knots tied together
felt like

something.

"Why are you here?"
Jordan asked.

Whatever it was in the haze of last night—
a heart poured over with alcohol,
emotions that betrayed me—
was nowhere to be found.

"You're his best friend."

      "You're his girlfriend."

"That's not how best friends
      are supposed to act."

Jordan snorted and shook his head.
He said nothing for a moment.

"Nothing is ever *supposed to* happen.
                Things just happen,"
                                he said.

"Was that all it was to you?"

        "You tell me."

"You're infuriating."

        "You're a bitch."

I wasn't going to be
the one who stood there
being shot at
like I was an orc on the screen.

"Good luck with your game!"
I shouted.

"And same to you,"
Jordan replied.

High school love

Was not supposed to end
the way mine did.
It was supposed to end
with the looming prospect of
college—

when separate schools,
quite possibly on separate coasts,
and the element of
time

could not possibly keep
two high school lovers
together.

Breaking up with Ben was supposed to occur
the summer before college, not
the summer before senior year.

Yet five months later, I still felt him
so rawly.

Ben's arms wrapped around my waist
like they belonged there,
like they hung there,
like the way sleeves belonged on a jacket.

Why I write #2
If I was to be branded,
as the girl who cheated
on her charismatic and lovable
boyfriend
with his best friend,
then I had to
become the person who
could at least make everyone pause
and for a moment
be someone
other than
that girl.

She cheated on her boyfriend,
but she's really fucking smart.
She cheated on her boyfriend,
but she got into Princeton.
She cheated on her boyfriend,
but she wrote my college essay
and now I'm going to
Duke.

We were all unbreakable
Audrey Pugh leaned against her locker,
angular hips protruding
like corners on a coffee table.
"I miss Ben," she said, pouting,
to Jilly, who snapped her gum
and wore her cheer skirt
in the off-season.

I missed him too,
so damn much.

"Ben was like the *nicest* guy
in our class. The *nicest*, Jilly."

Jilly's head bobbled.

I didn't know whether
to slow down or speed up.
To act totally oblivious,
or confrontational.

But then the choice was made for me.
"Nic," Audrey called out,
"I need your help."

I didn't understand why on earth

Audrey Pugh
would utter the word "help"
and my name
in the same sentence.

It was like she totally forgot
that time freshman year
when she told my mom
I was bulimic.
I wasn't. I'm not.

"I'm not a doctor yet, Audrey.
So it would be unethical of me
to diagnose
that rash on your ass."

Jilly's jaw dropped. Her gum nearly fell out.
Audrey's mouth tightened for a millisecond,
then relaxed like I had said
nothing at all.

Audrey was like this perfectly
unbreakable
twig,
the rubbery kind
that bows and bends
but never snaps.

Pavlov's dog

"I need you to write my college essay,"
Audrey said.
She thrust a wad of cash
in my face.
"I hear you do that sort of thing."

I could have said no.
I wasn't sure
I could write anything nice
or meaningful about Audrey Pugh.

Yet I snatched the cash
from her fingers
like I was conditioned to,
like Pavlov's dog,
and began counting the bills.

Audrey's mouth formed a small,
knowing smile.
"Oh, Nic.
It's just a wad of twenties.
Your family has money, right?
Or did your mother
take all of it
before she left?"
She laughed before shutting her locker

and trotting away
with Jilly.

There was nothing Audrey
could say
about my mother
that I haven't
heard before.

Rumors grew
lackluster
over time,
but they still
gnawed on
parts inside me.

Yet, in spite of all the terrible things
Audrey and I
have mutually said
to and about
each other,

I still wanted
to write
her essay.

Maybe it was
the way she existed
as a unit.

The way none of us
were ever quite sure
if either twin
were truly
different
from the other.

The way she shielded
her innermost feelings
and thoughts,
her own identity
so none of us
could see.

If I could write an essay
for Audrey,
then maybe
there was something
worth writing
about all of us.

There were papers
Papers covered
every inch of my room.

They insulated me
from thinking,
from feeling
too much.

Vignettes of Marco
and Miranda
and Laurel
and Austin,
lives that demanded
attention.

I was exhausted by
their words.

But of course,
I couldn't stop.

By December

The days felt fleeting.
Everything that you wanted to last longer—
lunch periods,
weekends,
the amount of time we were given on an
exam—
passed quickly.

Everything you wanted to fly by—
homework,
lectures,
winter itself—
only dragged slower.

Jordan tore a page
Out of his notebook
and flicked the crumpled paper
at me as we sat
across from each other
at a table in the crowded library,
cramming for upcoming exams.

I flicked the paper back.
"What do you want,
Jordan?"

He leaned back in his chair.
"That's the million-dollar
question.
Thanks for asking.

"My dad bought me a new Rover,"
he said.

"Good for you."
I went back to studying.

"Is that supposed to mean
love?"
Jordan mused.
His elbows leaned

on the table, his chin
resting in his hand.

"I don't know,"
I muttered.

Jordan continued to ramble
like I wasn't even there.
"Do you notice that no one ever asks
what you want?
Like I didn't ask for this Rover.

"Maybe I wanted an Audi.
Or maybe I just want
my dad to, like,
ask me about something
other than my GPA
and whether or not I finished
that Princeton application.

"Would have saved him $80K."

I stopped writing and put down my pen.

Our friendship may have ended
at his party last summer,
but there were invisible threads

of something
that I could still feel
tangling us
together.

"Maybe I would like to know
if my dad knows anything about me
other than my class rank,"
Jordan grumbled, opening up his textbook.

I returned to working
on the practice test
for AP Bio,
when Jordan said,
"When someone doesn't have an interest
in you,
you stop having an interest
in yourself."

I looked up at him.
"I get it."

"I know you do, Nic,"
Jordan whispered.
"Also, your answer to question seven
is wrong."

Early decision

We checked our phones obsessively.
Not for a text,
or a like,
or a friend request,
or a photo,
but for an e-mail,
with a .edu address,
preferably from an Ivy.

Suitors

A week before Christmas,
I found five guys
gathered around my desk
at the start of AP Bio.
They leaned over Jordan's shoulder,
saying things like,
"Shit, man" and
"That's so sick."

"Oh my.
Five strapping young suitors
have come a-calling,"
I said.
"What will I tell my mother?"

They glanced over at me,
then back at Jordan,
and then back at me.

"That's not why
you're here?"
I feigned a dramatic sigh
and stepped over
their backpacks.

"Move," I said,
and the five of them
scurried away.

Jordan swiveled around in his seat,
facing me.
His left arm was wrapped
in a hard cast
up to the elbow.
He swung it around in the air
like a giant mallet.

"Nicky, did you include
'Killer of fun'
and 'Where the party goes to die'
in your list of extracurricular activities
on your college application?
Because you sure excel at them."

I smirked back.
"What the hell did you do to your arm,
Jordan?"

"Nicky, that is an excellent question.
I thought you'd never ask."

He whipped out his phone and
cued up a video.

I mostly saw Ben,
or at least the outline of Ben,
on the screen from the vantage point
of a helmet-mounted camera.

They were in the mountains,
in the snow.
Ben, bundled up in a North Face jacket
zipped up to his nose.
Goggles and a helmet
covered the rest of his face.
But I could tell it was him.

I knew that nose.
The nose that
snuggled against mine.
The nose that
I would kiss ever so lightly
when saying good-bye.

My heart paused for a moment,
and then I felt a stab of anger.

Jordan was still friends
with Ben.
Still close enough
that Ben could drive into the mountains
and spend a whole day
with someone who slept
with his girlfriend.

There were girls
who I was never even friends with
who won't talk to me
because I cheated on Ben.

Yet Jordan
still gets to
live his normal life
as if nothing ever happened?

The double standard
was infuriating.

Jordan was
infuriating.

Roadkill

In the video, Ben took off first,
on his skis,
down what looked to be
a steep mountainside.
Jordan pointed the camera downhill.
You could see Ben
flying off a man-made jump
vaulted into the air,
crossing what now appeared to be
a mountain highway.

Ben sailed across it and landed
miraculously
on the other side of the road,
in the snow.

I turned to Jordan. "Are you guys idiots?"

Jordan nodded his head vigorously,
grinning.

You could hear Ben hollering
and Jordan saying something like,
"All right, watch this."
Famous last words.

I continued to watch and saw
the tip of Jordan's board
barrel down the hill.
He hit the jump
and for a moment
you saw the pavement below
as Jordan and his board sailed over.

Then you saw
the front edge of his board nick
the guardrail
on the other side of the road.

There was a blur of whiteness
accompanied by numerous expletives.
When the camera came to rest,
it was staring back at the face of Ben,
who was howling with laughter.
"That was fucking awesome,"
he said.

Then you could hear Jordan say,
with a hoarseness,
"I think I broke my wrist, man."

The video went black
and the screen asked us to replay.

I didn't need the video to replay.
It replayed on its own
in my mind.

Except this time
I imagined Ben flying off that jump,
soaring across that road.
I imagined an oncoming truck
barreling down the highway,
the way my imagination
kept barreling down
this horror.

I tried to make it stop,
and I did.

But the fear
of being cold
and alone
resurfaced,

and I imagined
the sight of roadkill,
on the side of
a snowy mountain highway.

To self-destruct

"What were you trying to do, Jordan?
Self-destruct?"
I said.

"Always," he replied,
turning back around in his seat,
and slipping his phone into a pocket.

I had this theory that our school was divided
into two types of people,
not between jocks and preps,
or honors and non-honors,
or popular and unpopular.

I had a theory that it was divided
by how we were programmed to live.
There were those of us like
Kitty, Ashok, and Laurel,
careful and contented,
pragmatic and happy.
They existed to wake up tomorrow,
always a new day,
because wasn't that the way we were
supposed to exist
as humans?
To keep living.

Then there are those of us who lived
differently.
Jordan, Miranda, and me.
We charged forward.
We took risks.
We strived for greatness
in every moment,
because every night we fell asleep thinking
this was it;
there wasn't going to be
a tomorrow.

But every morning
when the alarm clock went off,
we would lie in our beds,
shocked
that despite everything we did
the previous day
to run our bodies
into the ground,
we continued
to wake up.

Ben was one of us.
He hid it so well,
and I loved him

and I hated him
for being this way.

He pretended he was happy
when he was sad.
He pretended he didn't care
about anything,
not college,
not grades,
quite often
not even me.

He pretended everything
would magically work
in his favor.

He denied that he understood me at all.
"Why do you have to study all the time?
Why can't you come over?"
he would plead on the phone.

But he aced the same tests as me.
He studied when no one was looking.
He fretted about his future
when no one was around.
He worried about his worth

alone,
like the rest of us.

Self-destruction seeped from his pores.
I knew this because
I smelled it.

It was the bourbon and beer
that excreted from his skin
in the early-morning hours on a Sunday.

When he rolled over in bed
and opened his eyes
after a hard night of partying,
I wasn't the first thing he noticed.

For a brief moment
his eyes looked at me
with an expression of shock
that his own body was
still breathing,
his heart
still beating,
his eyes
still seeing.

Then Ben would smile awkwardly
and say,
"Morning, gorgeous."

I could have died
every time
he said that
with half-drunk, groggy eyes.

But I never did.

Cursors

I see my empty heart,
which blinks like a cursor
on a blank white screen,
waiting.

I try
typing words:

*I wish I could tell you why
I went up to that room
with Jordan.*

*I wish I could say
why I pine and pine
for you, Ben.*

*Is it enough to say
that the wanting
is the something
that holds me together?*

It's the hope that simmers.

But I stare at black marks
against a harsh white light

Juleah del Rosario

and like
nothing that I see.

I hit the backspace
until it becomes
a screen

of words unwritten,
of life unexpressed,

the moments we bury,
that feeling
we don't feel.

A cursor
because

what is more lonely
than a solitary cursor?

Best party ever forgotten
The new girl was having a party,
and I was there
with Kitty and Ashok.

People said it was *uh-mazing*.
That there were signature cocktails,
or rather mocktails,
because her parents were
making the drinks.

People said there was a DJ
in the basement
from the fancier school
with an endowment
that could support
a small country.

People said he was hot,
along with the other guys
the new girl invited
from her old school,
which I never realized
until just now
was the same school
that Ben transferred to.

"Holy shit,"
Kitty said.
Her hand flew over her mouth.
"Don't turn around, Nic."
But of course
I turned around.

"Ben,"
I breathed.

The last thing you wanted

Was for your ex-boyfriend to look
so damn good.

Looking so damn good

Ben in his jacket and tie
that made him look like
a proper young man,
the kind you took home to your parents,
the kind you snuck out of your house for,
the kind you ended up with,
for whatever forever means.

Ben with his floppy brown hair
pushed to the side,
which made him look
like he rolled out of bed,
effortlessly attractive,
effortlessly yours.

Ben with his coaxing half smile,
which you thought was saying,

Talk to me.

So that's what you decided
to do.

When I stared into his eyes

I was not getting the
I'm-so-happy-to-see-you-I-want-to-be-with-you
eyes.
I was getting something along the lines of
We're-at-the-grocery-store-and-we-ran-into-each-other-in-the-cereal-aisle-so-how-are-you
eyes.

"Hi."
I broke the ice.
Literally.
Jamming a straw
up and down
against frozen cubes
in a glass
filled with ginger ale
and shattered dreams.

"Nic. Hey.
How's the party?"
Ben said.

I could have asked him the same question.
I could have asked a million questions.

How are you?
What have you been up to?
Do you miss me?

But I stood there in front of him,
drinking from a now-empty glass
and gnawing on the end of a straw,
just staring and forgetting
that no words had come out.

His head tilted.
His brow furrowed.
"Are you okay?"
Ben asked.

Of course not.

"I'm great,"
I said.
I smiled.
I wish I felt
the realness of a smile
on my skin.
But I was numb.

He nodded tentatively.

I opened my mouth to say something else,
maybe to change the conversation,
maybe to say *I'm sorry*,
but I closed it again,
swallowing thick air.

Ben's eyes changed.
The tension he held on his brow melted.
In all the years I had known him,

I had never seen the expression
he now bared on his face.

It was like all the questions
had been answered.

It happened
Ben was in love.
And he wasn't looking at me.

She had pale skin,
auburn hair,
a crooked smile,
and slightly crooked teeth.

She was fucking
                adorable.

"Nic, this is . . . ,"
Ben began,
but I didn't want him
to finish the sentence.

I didn't give a shit what her name was.

I know

As I walked away
Jordan muttered,
"You can't have him back, Nic."

He stood at the edge of the room,
by the doorway
that led to the foyer,
that led to the front door.

"I know."
I more than knew.
I felt it.

It was like snuffing out a candle
with a pewter cone
and watching the smoke
curl around the underside
of my heart.
It was like smoke
slipping away
through my stomach.

"You were watching us?"
I said to Jordan.
"You knew about her?"

Jordan leaned arrogantly
against the doorframe,
like the transitional space
was his
to own.

But Jordan reached out
for my hand
and squeezed it
like it meant something,
and maybe it did, because
I exhaled, not realizing
I was holding
my breath.

"We broke him,
Nic,"
Jordan whispered.

And maybe
a small part of me
escaped.

Honda Civics

I folded over
like a ball of kneaded dough
in the backseat of
Kitty's Honda Civic.

"Um, what's going on back there?"
Ashok said to Kitty
from the passenger seat.

Passengers,
weren't we all just passengers
in life?

"Nic, are you okay?"
Ashok asked.

"I'm fine."
Fine, fine, fine, fine, fine.

"She's not fine,"
Kitty said.
"She saw her ex-boyfriend with . . ."

With that adorable fucking girl,
the girl Ben—my Ben—was in LOVE with.

"That girl is so basic,"
Ashok said.

"I can hear you.
I'm still back here."

Ashok turned around.
"Real talk, Nic.
You're so much more."

I was more than basic,
that's for sure.
More complicated,
more precarious,
more flawed.

Ashok turned back to face
the windshield.
"I hope you take that
as a compliment,
by the way."

Attempting not to text someone
I wanted, I wanted, I wanted
to text
Ben.

To say all the things
I should have said to him
at the party,
when we were together.

Kitty and I sat in my driveway
after dropping off Ashok,
the car still running
but me not wanting to move
from the backseat.

Kitty eyed me from the rearview mirror.
She knew everything.
She turned around.
She grabbed for my phone.
"Don't do it, Nic.
It's not worth it."

I loosened my grip.
The phone fell
into her hands.

"I miss him so much.
I love him."

She sighed.
"I know, Nic.
You might always love him."

The phone buzzed

I rolled over to check it.
I still wanted it to be Ben.
Every time.

Jordan.
Hey.

           Hi?

Come over.

           Why?

. . .

I watched until the screen went gray
and then black.
I set the phone down.
I rolled over.
I pulled a pillow over my face
so I wouldn't stare at the ceiling,
so I wouldn't wonder why
Jordan said, *Come over*,
at one in the morning.
Like I was his.

We should talk.

. . .

I got out of bed,
slid on a pair of jeans,
pulled a sweatshirt out of the laundry,
and put on a good bra—
the black lace kind.

The stalker
I opened the front door
to no parents,
no Jordan.

I slipped through the halls
and up the stairs
to where I remembered
his room.

He lay in his bed,
already asleep,
snoring, guttural.

I felt like a stalker
invading his space,
his privacy,
as I lay my head
on Jordan's chest.

How many of us knew
that Jordan breathed from his stomach
in spurts, in a struggle
between diaphragm and lungs?

It was like an old car shaking
with not enough gas.

I was wide-awake and listening,
and wanting
to know
why I was here.

But I knew
why he texted me,
why we were supposed
to talk.

I knew in the way
he squeezed my hand,
the way he breathed
unsteady.

I was here
because we broke
Ben,
and in doing so,
we may have
broken
ourselves.

I listened
to Jordan sleep.

At some point, something
rattled loose.
The struggle was over.
His chest rose and fell, steady
breathing
like a normal person.

Silence lingered

In the morning,
I listened for signs of life.
Dishes being unloaded.
Voices hushed or hummed.
Bare soles plodding on hardwood.
Coffee grinding.

All I heard was Jordan.
The air pushing
its way through his nostrils
into his chest
into his lungs
and back out again.

Jordan slept,
and I untangled myself
from the sheets.

I picked my clothes
off the floor,
clothes that landed there
after Jordan awoke
in the middle of the night
and found me
curled next to him.

When we held each other
fiercely.
When we wanted so badly
to feel.

I fished under the bed,
as I had done before,
for a shirt,
and slipped out of his room.

Downstairs, nothing
looked like the Parker house
I remembered.

Unopened mail
lay in toppled stacks.

Dishes
remained unwashed.

A wall clock
with an hour hand
stuck between twelve and one.

There were signs
of family,

but no one
was home,

except Jordan,
alone.

I knew the sound
of silence
that lingered
in the halls
of an empty home.

And for a moment I felt
like my heart was a sponge for sadness,

but then I saw the thing
that would wring it all out.

On the refrigerator
hung a letter
with an orange and black crest
that I knew too well.

It began as all the letters
I had imagined would begin,
all the letters I imagined finding
in my in-box,

in my mailbox,
on my own fridge.

We are delighted . . .
it said, and I didn't need to read
any further.

Jordan Parker had Princeton.
Jordan Parker had fucking
        everything.
Jordan Parker had
        me.

Deferred

Dear Ms. Chen,

We received a record number of early-decision applications this year, many of which are of great quality, yet we only choose to admit a small percentage of students from the early-decision pool.

Your application will be deferred, and reviewed again in the regular-decision pool.

Expect to hear a final response in late March or early April.

Warm regards,

Princeton Dean of Admissions

Counting Christmases

Xiaoling had been with us
for two Christmases
and she had already mastered

how to power shop
on Christmas Eve
at the Meydenbauer Mall,

how to discreetly buy me a present
and slip it into her purse
before I could even see
what it was.

For two Christmases
I had eaten home-cooked meals
with a family different
from the one I started with
seventeen years ago,

and maybe this was because
I used to have a mother
who drank a bottle of Riesling
and passed out under the tree
while Dad and I ate pepperoni pizza
three Christmases ago.

What I knew about my mother's disappearance
I knew she packed one rolling suitcase.
I knew she cleaned out her half
of the bank account.
I knew the police were never called.
I knew Dad filed divorce papers.
I knew Mom signed them
somehow.
How . . . ?

What I suspected
She ran away with another man,
because
I could hear her
talking to someone,
in a voice that sounded
like a growl
on the nights
when Dad
worked late.

What I also suspected
was that Dad
knew exactly
where she was.

But no one
seemed to care
that I
did not.

What I sometimes thought
She didn't love me.

How could she,
if she hadn't even called
or written
or come back
for her daughter?

I felt things falling
Like ornaments slipping off
branches on a Christmas tree,
when glass baubles
hit the floor
and shatter,
like I've lost.

PART II:
Acceptance

Second Semester Senior Year

I thought we would all catch
senioritis.

But the kid in front of me
in AP Calculus
quietly banged his head
against the desk
as our teacher explained
a particularly challenging problem set.

"That's not going to help you
on the exam,"
Miranda muttered.

I desperately wanted
the epidemic
of senioritis
to sweep through the halls
of Meydenbauer
and put us all
out of our misery.

Deadlines

Laurel and Austin and everyone
who wanted an essay
whispered, "Where is it, Nic?"
"Where's my essay, Chen?"
when I took a seat next to them
in class.

Miranda leaned over
and whispered.
"It's January, Nic.
Applications are due
in two weeks."

"Stanford, Nic. Stanford,"
Miranda reminded me,
as if I didn't know.

"I will destroy you
if you fuck this up."
She leaned so close
the words permeated
my skin.

Miranda's essay was finished.
All of them were,
beautifully written.

It was inevitable
that in writing
with so much truth
pieces of me
would be woven
between the lines
of each essay.

To hand them over
would be handing over
pieces of myself,
and I wasn't quite ready
to let go.

A Draft of Miranda Price's Essay

Nobel Laureate and Professor of Physics Stefan Stanovnik once said, "We used to see chaos in nature, until we found new tools that showed us order. Our perspective on randomness has shifted dramatically." Tell us about a time your perspective changed and what has shifted in your understanding of the world.

I raise my hand high in all my classes, especially in science and math. I have been elected to student government all four years of high school. I used to not understand the concept of a "glass ceiling" or an "achievement gap." I used to think that I was not any different from my male peers. I used to believe we were all equals—high-achieving, driven, and confident.

Then I went viral on YouTube.

Perspective changes when one's face is streaming online with more than forty thousand views. Parents look at you differently. Their eyes are a constant source of disappointment. All the guys at school stare at you differently. The girls, they don't look at you. They talk about you.

What happened that night was me at a party, dancing in an outfit I liked, laughing with friends I adored, and admittedly wearing heels that were too high and too precarious for feet that are prone to clumsiness. I fell flat on my face, and that is the extent of what happened.

If the video were simply me tripping over my own feet or something equally careless, I could laugh it off and nothing would have changed. But it's not.

Somewhere out in the crowd someone was filming me. With the music and editing and snippets of me saying things out of context, this isn't a video of a clumsy girl falling. It is a gut-wrenching portrayal of how others—specifically, my male peers—see me.

The video is textbook "male gaze," as coined by Laura Mulvey. I know this from the film studies course I took at the university the summer after sophomore year. I wrote an entire paper on the use of the male gaze in contemporary horror films, analyzing the way camera angles fetishized women, even in their death. I understood the male gaze that summer, as it related to film theory, but I did not comprehend the insidious way it could impact my life.

Now I do. When I watch the video of myself, I see me, but I am forced to experience the moment, not as I remember, but instead through the misogynist and scopophilic perspective of my male peers. There's an ass shot. The video lingers on parts of my body. You can hear guys talking about me, critiquing me, my dance moves, and scoring my eventual fall.

As much as I feel like an equal, I am not. I cannot turn the camera around on those guys, shoot the same video with the same shots and upload it to YouTube, expecting the same results. I am so frustrated and at times so angry, but I am still so driven and confident.

I still serve on student government. I raise my hand in all my classes. I still go to parties and dance and wear heels too high. But it's different now. There's a part of me that wonders if I will ever be seen as who I am.

It was still senior year
I stood alone
in front of my locker, staring
back at those
fucking letters.

Someone had decided to write WHORE
on my locker
again.

Ben had moved on.
Yet I didn't get to?
My reputation didn't get to progress
to something more favorable?

Like maybe, just maybe,
could someone write
SMART
or
INTELLIGENT
or
TALENTED
in bright orange lipstick
on my locker?

A figure darted
down the empty hall.

Of course.

"Jordan!"

He paused.
He saw me.
He slumped his shoulders
and disappeared,

like the way he disappeared,
along with Ben,
after his party
last summer.

How had I become
the girl
who everyone
runs away
from?

"Nic, don't."
Kitty materialized.

"Don't what? Call out to him?
Chase after him?
Sleep with him
again?"

Jordan didn't call.
He didn't text.
He did nothing to acknowledge
what happened
between us,
again,
that night
over winter break
when

the rain pattered against the window
and the wind grabbed hold of the trees,
when I crawled into his bed
and he wanted me.

"I didn't . . . ,"
Kitty began.

I didn't stick around
long enough to hear
what Kitty had to say.

Foot over foot pounded
the glossy linoleum floor.

But in the distance
I could hear her say,

"What the hell, Nic?
I'm your friend.

"That means something."

But I was too far gone
to let those words
sink in.

"Jordan!"
I called out.
"Jor—dan!"

It was like
his name echoed incessantly
in my brain—rattling around.
Bouncing off walls.
Ricocheting.

But it wasn't in my head.
It was loud and clear
for everyone to hear.

I was
that girl.

The one calling after her—

what?

What do I even call Jordan?
My friend?
What kind of shitty friendship
was this?

Definitely not my lover.
This wasn't fucking love.

It was—
and I stopped.

As all the doors around me closed,
one finally opened,
and a boy stepped into
the hall.

Ben

"I transferred back, Nic."

No.
I closed my eyes. Squeezed them hard.
Willed everything in my brain
to smother the image of Ben.

He was still there
when my eyes opened again,
nodding and standing
in front of me.

It was like reality
had shape-shifted
itself into this horrible
creature
with three heads
and tentacles
wrapped around my chest,
compressing what little
sense of self
I had.

My heart wanted to crawl
into bed with Ben
and entangle every

ventricle with his.
It wanted to spill red
on this linoleum floor
and bleed and bleed and bleed.

It wanted to stop pounding
for a moment
and just
be still.

"I missed this place,"
Ben said.

He glanced around.
"Jordan said nothing
has changed.

"He was right."

"Except us,"
I said.

"Yeah—I mean there's that."

Ben stood there,
cocking his head,

with eyes that gazed
right through me.

He could have melted my heart
in a million different ways,
but this time
he broke it

like I was porcelain
falling on a marble floor.

Again

The world felt like it was on fire,
but it was raining
again.

The halls were abuzz
With Ben.

I heard his name
in hushed tones
during class.
He darted past
my line of sight
on more than one occasion.

Ben was back,

and I thought
that would mean
my life could go
back to normal.

But now
Ben was back,
and nothing really changed.

People jostled me,
they knocked into
my book bag,
they looked up
occasionally

and muttered,
"Sorry."

As the bell rang,
I saw a hundred people
pass me by
and I felt
so alone.

"You look
like the saddest
damn puppy
in the pound."

I took a deep breath
of the stale hallway air
and turned to Ashok.

"Second semester
is rough,"
was all I could muster.

He nodded.
"Shit just got real,
but let's go crush this class."

There were no extra seats
In AP Bio
for our newest classmate,
our transfer student,
our Ben,
who sat in the back
at a lab table
among the pestles and pipettes.

From the back of the room
Ben could stare
into the back of my head,
watch as I took notes,
or pretend I didn't exist,
that the months we spent
with interlaced fingers
never happened.

Maybe he had to.
Maybe we both did.

Jordan walked in late,
per usual.
He slid into his seat
without catching my eye.

I didn't know what happened
or what was happening
or what would happen
between Jordan and me.

We were both furniture
with missing bolts,
wobbling just enough
that when you got close to us,
you would know
something
was not right.

Minutes hurled us forward
like an airplane
on a runway,
wheels on the ground,
never quite lifting,
never aloft,
as we approached
college application
deadlines.

January 14

Texts hit me like a hailstorm.

Yo. Where's my essay?
Nic, are you still writing my essay?
Can you send over that essay
I PAID YOU FOR?
You realize applications are due
TOMORROW.

I sat on a glossy floor
in an empty hallway
before school started,
laptop resting on my thighs,
ready to cue up the essays
and send a series of e-mails.

Then Ben walked by.
"'Sup, Nic."
He head-nodded.

And before Ben was even
out of sight,
I had forgotten all about the texts,
all about the essays,
all about the deadlines,
all about anything

and anyone
in this world
except

a boy
with floppy brown hair
and eyes
that looked like
storm clouds
and choppy waters
and torrential downpours
soaking into my heart.

At home alone

I had to keep writing. Compulsively.

I found myself typing
and feeling
and typing
and feeling
too many things all at once.

I found myself stringing
words I had written
together.
Words that would mean
something to someone.
Words that could
feel
too many things all at once.

I found myself
attaching documents
to e-mails,
attaching aspirations
to essays,
and clicking send
over and over again
as I dulled
in the bright white light.

In response
To the essays
I had painstakingly crafted,
Miranda sent an e-mail
that read,
About fucking time,
Chen.

A single sheet of paper
Slipped out of my locker
and fluttered down to
the linoleum floor,
recently waxed and shiny.

Kitty held the sheet,
scanning through,
brow beginning to furrow.

She read through the essay
about Miranda or Audrey,
Marco or Austin.
It didn't really matter who.

"You know what doesn't make sense,
Nic?
It's not that this is clearly wrong,
or that you charged a shit ton
of money
when you don't even need it.

"It's that you would invest so much,
be so thoughtful,
take the time
to get to know somebody

you don't even
care about."

Kitty paused.
She looked down at the essay.
"It's like you cared
more about these essays,
than you did about
our own friendship.
It hurts, Nic."

She handed me the single sheet of paper
before walking away,

leaving me in a familiar hallway
with familiar doors
and familiar lockers
and familiar faces
that sauntered by.

But Kitty walked away,
leaving me in a place
unfamiliar.

Dislodged

I held the sheet of paper,
slightly crumpled.

Austin's essay.

Austin who I
barely spoke to.
Austin who I didn't
really know.

Austin whose place
next to Jordan
dislodged
when Ben reappeared.

That night I slept with Jordan,
the first time,
something also dislodged.

Kitty was right.

From the safety
of an emotional distance
I could write
about people
I barely knew.

But with her,
with Jordan,
with Ben,
with myself,

I couldn't even ask
the right questions
to dig deeper
into knowing
who we were.

A Draft of Austin Schroeder's Essay

Discuss an accomplishment, event, or experience that generated a new understanding of yourself.

When I went onstage as Willy Loman, I entered into an implicit agreement with the audience that they would see me, not as a sixteen-year-old sweaty soccer player or the taciturn physics whiz, but as a man of sixty or so years, carrying the weight of an underwhelming life in his briefcase. I asked them to believe who I was in that moment, and in turn I would deliver them that man.

The soccer guys were shocked when I forwent winter training in favor of trying out for the school play, and even more confused when I landed the lead male role in *Death of a Salesman*. My castmates were intrigued, as I had never set foot in the theater and had no formal training like the rest of them. They called me a "natural" and a "quick study."

But when I went onstage as Willy Loman, I knew what to do more acutely than the way I knew how to find the open space on a soccer field, or the way I knew that the answer to problem set seven in AP Physics was $\Delta t = 5s$. I knew how to perform.

I had been performing my whole life, and I was good at it. I had nailed the role of "Soccer Stud," down to the calculated days that I didn't wash my hair. I had perfected the lie of effortless intelligence, pretending I was "out with a girl" instead of at home reading and rereading textbooks. I delivered on those roles, and the audience—everyone around me—loved me for it.

But after the curtain fell on *Death of a Salesman* and I took my final bow, who was I asking the audience to believe I was now?

Sometimes an actor goes so deep into a role that when he emerges, he no longer knows who he is. He cannot divorce himself from the role he perfected. Sometimes I feel like I have been performing for too long and can no longer divorce myself from the act.

But a funny thing happened after I became Willy Loman. I could start to be someone my friends no longer recognized. I could be someone who washed his hair every day, or never washed it at all. I could be someone who studied seventeen hours for the physics final and wasn't ashamed to share.

I could slowly be myself, whoever that was—a self no longer onstage.

Loneliness
Isn't this gaping hole
in your heart
because your boyfriend
broke up with you.

It isn't being dateless
on prom night.

It isn't even
the emotional distance
between you
and your parents.

Loneliness is living
in your own skin
with a person
you don't even know.

Loneliness is
the void of self,
the absence of knowing
who you are.

We waited

We waited for exams to be graded
and classes to end.

We waited for ski season
to turn into prom season.

We waited for our lives to change
with a single e-mail
from a university
that wanted us.

Weeks went by
and nothing changed

until it did.

We no longer waited
Meydenbauer continued to function
like the gears in an old watch,
with classes,
and lunches,
and passing periods
ticking by.

Then the letters
began to roll in.

I stood by my locker
and watched a stream
of oversize T-shirts
parade through the doors
announcing each chosen
school.

Santa Barbara and Santa Clara,
Cornell and Bucknell,
Seattle U and Wash U.

I had a letter.
A weighty envelope.
An e-mail from a .edu,
a crest in orange and black ink.

We are delighted . . . ,
it began.

I was in.

Somehow,
we all were in.

"I heard you got into Princeton!"
Ashok said
as we walked to class.

I nodded.

"And that you got
Miranda into Stanford,
Marco into RISD,
Laurel into Brown,"
he whispered.

I shrugged.

"Congratulations, Nic.
You are a freakin' dream maker!"
Ashok patted me on the back.

"Whatever," I said, and shrugged.

Ashok lurched forward
and stopped.

"Oh, hell no, Nic.
You do not get to
whatever me.

"We are friends,
and I'm here
trying
to be that person.
But what kind of person
are you
trying
to be?"

I looked Ashok dead
in the eye.
"I don't know," I said.

Ashok turned to face me.

"You are the girl who got into Princeton.
You are the girl who got everyone else
into their dream schools.
You are the girl who
changed people's lives."

"But I'm still the girl
who cheated on her boyfriend,
the girl who cheated
on those essays,
the girl who cheated

because maybe
that's who I am."

"Do you really believe that, Nic?"

"I don't know,"
I said again.

Bryant Barnett walked by
wearing an Elbridge College shirt.
He smiled wide and gave us
two thumbs-up.

I thought about the essay
I didn't write,
the words of Bryant Barnett.
"The most whole,"
I whispered.

Ashok nodded excitedly.
"Yes! We are people
trying
to be
the most whole."

I thought
It was Ben's heart
that was buried
in a cold storage locker,
with the meats and the cheeses
and the emotions he never brought out
to thaw

when we were together.

But I was beginning to think
that it might have been
my own.

Guilt is an internal state
We make mistakes
that sleepwalk
with us,

and guilt is a kind of sadness
that can sleep
for months,

until we awake
and roll over in bed
with guilt

there
to change us.

I gave everything
To those essays
and I felt like shit.

"Do you feel guilty?"
I stopped Miranda
in the hall.
I flung the question at her.

She furrowed her brow.
She still towered over me.
"Sometimes."
She shrugged.

"For using my essay,"
I said.

Miranda rolled her eyes.
She hitched her bag higher.
"I didn't use your essay.

"God, Nic.
I'm valedictorian,
clearly not an idiot."

"Huh?"
I said.

"It wasn't a complete waste
to pay you.

"What you wrote about me,
it was surprisingly
truthful.

"You wrote
the version of me
that has always
been there,
but I never saw.

"That essay
helped me see myself
as who I am,
who I will be.

"But you think I'd risk
Stanford
by submitting
your essay?

"Hell no.

"I wrote another one.
About my volunteer trip to Haiti.
I guess they liked it."
She smirked.

Did you use my essay?
I texted.

It was dope. Thnx,
responded Austin.

Um. No. Sorry!
responded Marco.

It was beautiful and thoughtful.
I loved it, Nic.
But no. I couldn't do it.
I felt too guilty,
Audrey wrote back.

Audrey continued to type.

. . .

And delete.

. . .

And type.

Because the three dots

clung to the screen
for far too long.

Also . . .
My sister would hate me forever,
so like please do not say ANYTHING
But . . .
I'm really really sorry
for what she did.
You know.
On your locker.

She didn't mean it.
She's kinda obsessed.
Like OBSESSED
with Jordan.
And well . . .

Good luck with everything
next year, Nic!

Jenny Pugh was a bitch.
She called me a whore
and smeared it
on my locker,

and I should
hate her
for it.

But a small part of me
was beginning to see
that we all weren't so different
from each other.

To everyone else,
we were all
a bitch, a whore,
a lover, a cheater,
a quarterback, a nerd.

But we weren't.
We were none of those words.
We were so much more.

After writing Audrey's and Austin's,
Miranda's and Marco's
and Laurel's essays,

after so much time
trying to feel
what it's like to walk
these halls
as someone else,

I could at least now see
that Jenny Pugh
was someone more.

A Draft of Audrey Pugh's Essay

Describe a person who has had a significant influence on you.

There are very few people in my life who would believe that I can hear my twin's thoughts, that I can feel what she feels in the blood that pumps through my heart. It sounds kooky and unscientific. Maybe it's not to those of us who were born into life with womb-mates. I love my sister, Jenny, to pieces. She is more than my best friend; she is my other half. If it were just the two of us, the world would be perfect.

There is more to this world than us. Last summer, when we traveled around Europe with our mother, I saw the way the young Spaniards, Frenchmen, and Dutchmen would gaze in her direction as she laughed boisterously without a sense of volume or care. Around town, I see the way she charms the ladies at the tennis club and the barista at the coffee shop who always "forgets" to charge her for an extra shot. I can feel her wanting to consume the world and the way the world wants to consume her.

Jenny is not going to college. She's told me this a million times. She's told our parents she's taking a gap year, in London or New York, where she'll go to make it in whatever "it" is. I can feel what the world wants from Jenny, but without her, what do I want from the world?

I once read an interview with the unknown twin sister

of a supermodel. The unknown twin chose to go to college, then law school, instead of New York Fashion Week and Milan like her sister. She described her sister as the sun, burning bright and radiant, and she as the moon, full and clear. I always thought I was destined to be the moon, the lesser-known twin, full and clear instead of burning bright. But with Jenny, I know what it feels like to shine bright.

Yet is it possible to have a world with two suns?

One night while in the south of France, Jenny and I sat on the terrace of a *maison* we were inhabiting for the week. The air was cool. Frogs croaked somewhere in the distance. The moon was there with us.

Jenny mused about a future gallivanting around Europe and jet-setting alone. I wanted her to want to take me with her, to want me by her side. But I let her continue to dream about a life where we were separable. Then she sighed, looked up at the sky, and said, "I love how the stars are a sun in someone else's world."

I know that we can both be suns in our own worlds, and that there's a world for me to find, and consume and be consumed by, with Jenny pumping through my heart.

Outside

Spring leaves held strong
on agitated branches
and fluttered,
like my heart that lay agitated
and fluttered
and tried to find a rhythm of solace,
but wasn't quite sure
if it should.

Like shattered glass

Late Saturday afternoon,
while I was studying for AP exams,
my phone lay dormant
on top of a textbook.

Then
the phone *ping*ed

like shattered glass.

A text from Ben
stared back at me.

I need you,
it said.

I froze.

Ben's number
*ping*ed again.

Everything slowly began
collapsing in
on itself.

It's Jordan,
it said.

And my heart
stopped.

To pretend to know what happened
According to the phone log
I had texted Jordan back.
I had texted him back as if he were Ben.
I had texted him with everything I ever
wanted to say

                    to Ben.

I miss you.
I love you.
I hurt you.

I'm sorry.

None of that mattered.
None of my texts were returned
by Ben

ever,

like the silence
that lingered on an empty street,
long after he drove away,
tires screeching around a corner.

The rain had returned
Like it always did
after I left Jordan's house
that evening.

It soaked through my jacket, my clothes,
into my skin.

I walked down barren sidewalks
listening
for the rumble of a skateboard,
the sound of a boy,
a sign of something
that might be
Ben.

Early this morning
they were in the mountains
spring skiing.
Ben and Jordan.

The powder was epic.
They took two different lines.
Ben handed Jordan his phone
for a photo.

What they couldn't see
was the water that trickled
into the fissures in the snow,
loosening the base.

If I closed my eyes,
just for a moment,
I could see Ben,
up there, on that mountain,
the one that peeked through the tops
of the evergreens.
I could see his long swooping tracks
writing cursive in the snow.

I could see
Ben looping down
the side of the mountain
one last time
before the roar of white powder
engulfed him.

My father sat
On a decorative bench
that no one ever used
under an awning
outside our front door.

Dad was here,
buried in the folds
of layers of Gore-Tex,
watching the rain,
waiting.

Tears streamed down my face.
Rain soaked into my shoes.
I wiped the snot away.

"Your friend was killed," my father said.
"It was on the news."

His voice was hollow and distant,
and he knew that I knew.

But he was
trying.

I went to open the front door.
"Xiaoling has dinner for you

on the stove,"
he said, and followed me inside.

My father never said much.
He couldn't fully understand.

The chasm between us
was always
too great.

But he was here.
He had always been here.

When Mom was pregnant and unmarried.
When Mom was erratic and unkind.
When Mom was nowhere to be found.
My father never left me.

Teenagers didn't die in avalanches
They died in
car crashes,
drunk-driving accidents,
drug overdoses,
gunshot wounds,
or suicide.

Their lives did not end
as arbitrarily
as getting caught
in Mother Nature's wrath.

I spent hours in front of
the computer, alone
in my room.
I obsessively googled everything
about avalanches.

According to the experts,
a beacon, a snow probe,
a shovel, a helmet
are good precautionary measures,

but no matter the gear,
the force alone
of snow

sliding down a mountain
can kill you.

According to the experts,
in an avalanche
one suffocates after being trapped
in the snow
for thirty minutes.

In an avalanche,
you have a whole half hour of life
to think about
whether this was going to be the end,
or whether someone was minutes away
from digging you out.

I wanted to believe
that in those thirty minutes
we all would try to live.

That we would claw
at the coalescing crystals,
and we would struggle
until we couldn't struggle anymore
to dig ourselves out,
already buried
six feet under.

A twig snapped
A branch fell.
Ben still died.

I wrote the essays.
I didn't get caught.
Ben still died.

We got into Stanford.
We got into Princeton.
But who the fuck cares?

Ben still died.

Death happens

Death doesn't give a fuck.
Death doesn't care
who is left behind.
Death doesn't care
if apologies were ever issued.
Death doesn't care
about the status
of your relationship.

Death will just happen.
But so will life.
Life will just happen.

But here's the other thing:
Life doesn't care
if you ever apologize,
if you do the wrong thing,
if you continue
to screw up,
if your moral compass
remains broken.

Life doesn't care either,
but you do.

You care.

The last time

Jordan, Ben, and I
were all together
before that night—
before Jordan had a party,
before the sound of tires
screeching around a corner—
we went swimming
at Meydenbauer Beach.

The sun was down, but the sky was still
light.

Jordan jumped off the dock first,
of course.
He did a single backflip in the air
before his entire body
came crashing down
to the lake.

Ben took a running start,
launched himself off the dock,
hugged his legs,
and somersaulted twice
in the air
before hitting the water.

Juleah del Rosario

I ran and leapt like the boys.
Once airborne, my legs kept pumping
as if trying to outrun
the sky.

Momentum died quickly,
and force pulled me down.

Water slapped
against my skin, as if to punish
us for trying so hard
to defeat the gravitational pull.

We bobbed and backstroked
our way along the lakeshore
until we ended up
in front of my house.

"Want us to drop you off here?"
Jordan asked.

No lights were on.
I felt the loneliness
that waited for me
inside.

"Nah. I'll swim back to the car

with you guys,"
I said.

And we backstroked our way
in the moonlight
beneath the materializing stars,
back to the public dock
and public beach
where we had left the car.

Nothing happened
that night.

We jumped. We swam.
We floated in the lake.

Nothing was perfect.
Nothing was right.

The woman who stood in front of me

On Sunday, the day after Ben died—

was killed in an avalanche,
froze to death,
suffocated in the snow,
whatever it was that happened,
suddenly,
tragically,
cruelly—

the doorbell rang.

The sound reverberated
off the sterile, marble
foyer.

The doorbell rang again
and again,
and no one seemed to want to answer it.

So I got up from my desk,
an unsuccessful attempt at doing homework,
and plodded over to the front door.

I opened it.

The woman who stood in front of me
wasn't supposed to be here.

Mom?
I mouthed the word slowly.

Her nails were unmanicured,
her blondish-gray hair uncoiffured.
She looked different, yet the same.
She looked like the person who was
supposed to be
my mom.

She reached across the threshold
into our house
and wrapped her arms around me,
not saying a word.

The rain came down like pellets,
drumming against the roof.

The rain came down like pellets,
drumming against her back.

The rain came down.

It was too much.

The way she touched me.
The way my skin felt safe.
The way I wanted to be in her arms
instinctively.

But I wanted nothing of it.
I hurt,

so much,

in that place wedged behind the heart.

I cried.
Big, fat tears,
like the rain outside.

"What
are you
doing
here?"
I knew why she was here,
but I needed to hear her answer.

"I heard.
About your friend.
Your dad called.
He was concerned.

I was concerned."

"Dad
called you?
He has
your *number*?

"You were *concerned*?

"You can't do this to me.
You can't just walk back into my life
after two years
when you walked out
without a note,
a phone number,
a good-bye."

I closed my eyes
so I could
breathe.

I didn't want to be here,
in this doorway,
with my mother,
under these circumstances.

It wasn't fair.

I didn't want Ben to
die
just so I could get my mother
back.

That wasn't the trade I was willing to make
in life.

My mouth opened
and two years' worth of words
came tumbling out.

Chunks of anger,
hurt,
loneliness.

"The boy I loved
dies,

"and you think
now
is a good time
to reappear?

"You don't suddenly
get to be
my mother."

"I had to leave.
I couldn't be here for you.
How am I supposed to love you
if I can't love myself?"
she said.

"You just are.
You are
my
MOM."

My heart fell onto
the floor,
and I was staring
at it,

beating.

The other woman
Xiaoling walked into the foyer.
She shook her head
and clicked her tongue.
Tsk, Tsk, Tsk.

She herded our bodies
out of the doorframe
and into the house,
then closed the door behind us.
She shuffled back into the kitchen.
A few minutes later
she reappeared
with a tray of cookies and tea.
"Come sit,"
she commanded.

Xiaoling was tiny
in comparison to my mother.
Her voice was not boisterous.
Her hair did not radiate
for miles away.
But she was fierce,
intense,
in charge,

just like my mother.

We followed.

Drinking with your mother

We sat in the living room
on the stark white
Egyptian cotton couch
that no one ever sat on.

Xiaoling poured us each
a cup of tea
and set them on top
of porcelain saucers.
She quietly left the room.

I watched my mom cool
her tea with her breath,
place the cup to her lips,
and sip
slowly.

I watched the hot water
evaporate off
the top of the teacup,
curling around in the air
before its shape
no longer existed.

I wondered if that was what
Ben's soul looked like

as it melted away
from the snow.

Did it seep out,
curl around in the air,
before—poof—
he was dead?

I knew

"Why did you leave?"
I finally said
the words
I needed to say.

Mom shook her head.
She held the teacup
close to her chest.
"Not now, honey."

I closed my eyes,
imagining the world
without Ben,
remembering
all the words
I never said.

"Mom, you abandoned me.
You walked away
from my life.
You tried to run away
from being a mother.

"You stopped
loving me,"
I said.

Tears crawled
down my cheek.

Mom set down her teacup.
"I never stopped loving you."

"Then tell me why
you disappeared."

She drew a long breath.
"I made a lot of mistakes, Nic."

"Yeah, you left me,"
I said.

"I thought it was harmless at first.
Coffee in the middle of the day,
in broad daylight,
in places where people knew us.
I thought it was all okay
because the sun was still out."

"Who?"
I said.

"You really don't need to know."

"But what if I do?"

Mom sighed.
"Fathers of people you know,
and men you never met."

I nodded. I knew this.
We all did,
if we chose to believe
the rumors
that spread around town.

"But it was never harmless.

"I wanted to feel like
someone loved me
as the woman I wanted
to be.

"I wanted that
more than wanting your father,
more than wanting to be
your mother,

"and I did anything
to have that."

I studied my mother's sagging eyes.
She was wrong.

At seventeen years old
I had learned
that we couldn't be
the person we wanted to be.

We can only be
who we are.

"You deserve a mother who—"

I stopped her.
"I deserve a mother."

My mother is a pine needle

My mother is cold air
stabbing you
in the chest,
in your lungs.

My mother is bright orange lipstick
scrawled on a locker, vying
to break me.

My mother is a pine needle
trapped between the windshield
and the wiper blade.

But my mother
is still
my mother.

Eleven weeks

It had been eleven weeks
since Ben died.

We all continued to show up to class.
We sat through our AP exams.
Some of us sent in deposits
for college tuition.

But nothing else was the same
at Meydenbauer.

Passing periods became
a quiet shuffle of feet down a hall.
Weekends dulled.
The excitement of graduation
was reserved for parents and family,
while us seniors approached it
with apprehension and
a sense of relief.

For eleven weeks
Jordan continued to slide
into his seat in front of me
in AP Bio.

Neither of us saying anything.
Both of us averting our eyes.

But I wanted us
to no longer be broken.
I wanted to superglue
all of our broken pieces
back together.
I wanted to tighten
the loose screws.

I wanted us to change.

What Jordan carried
Jordan padded down the hall
wearing Ray-Bans affixed
to his face since the funeral.

He carried an unzipped bag
with papers and notebooks
and textbooks falling
at his side.

He kept moving,
not even acknowledging
his lighter load.

"Jordan, your shit
is coming out of your backpack.
You are literally leaving
a trail of homework
down the hall,"
I said, following behind,
gathering up
the debris.

He stopped.
I handed him back
his things.

Jordan stuffed the papers
and books
back into his bag.
"It's not the person
that haunts you,
or the regrets,"
he said.

He zipped up his bag
and continued talking
as if talking
to no one
in particular.

"It's the arbitrariness of death.
The searching and searching
in the weeks and months
that follow
for some sort of
meaning."

He paused.

"I wake up every morning
and there's a feeling
in my stomach that says

it's different now,"
he continued.

"But I can't make sense
of what different means."

Jordan and I
had known each other
for years,
and I thought
I knew him.

But when I looked at Jordan today,
a week before graduation,
his face slightly puffy,
his left shoulder sagging,
his button-down shirt
wrinkled and worn
with the scent of musk
and perspiration,

I saw him as he was.

A young man
scared,
anxious,

confused,
sometimes desperate,
often lonely,
beneath an air of bravado.

"We fucked up royally, Nic,"
Jordan said.

Acceptance

"Did you know
that we are the only two students
in the entire region
who were admitted to Princeton?"
Jordan asked.

I shook my head.

"The acceptance rate is 6.4 percent
with thirty-one thousand applicants,
and the only other person
admitted to Princeton
from the area
is you, Nic.

"Of course it's you."
Jordan continued.

"The girl I slept with.
The girl who dated
my best friend,
my best friend
who died.

"Don't you think
we both got accepted

out of some sick joke?
A cruel form of karma?"

"That's not how college admissions work,"
I said.

"But isn't it kind of
a crapshoot
to be admitted
to an Ivy?

"Like, don't they just
throw all our applications
on the floor
and pluck two off the ground
and stamp them with
'Admit'?"

"No,"
I said.

Not everything
in life
was arbitrary.

Jordan shrugged.

"Jordan, you have a 4.0 GPA.
National Merit Finalist.
Class president for three years."

"My father bought my acceptance.
He donated handsomely to the school,"
Jordan said.

I didn't say anything.

"Well, good thing he spent all that money
to ensure my spot at Princeton,
because I just sent in my deposit
to UW yesterday,"
Jordan continued.

"You're staying here?"
I asked.

"Yep."

"Why?"

"Because I was always supposed to go
to Princeton.
Because I was supposed to become
my father,

and my father is an asshole,"
Jordan said.

His voice softened.
"Because I will never find out
who I am
if I go to Princeton."

Jordan stopped talking. He bit his lip.

"Did you know that Ben called me
only four days after
the night of my party?"
Jordan asked.

I shook my head.

"He called me to say,
'Dude, it's okay.
We're gonna be okay,'"
Jordan continued.
"We were never the same,
but we were something,
and Ben made that happen."

Jordan's eyes started to well.
"I don't know why

Ben forgave me, Nic.
But he saw something inside me
that was worth
forgiving."

Tears streamed down my face.
I stood there and let them fall.

I will never know
if Ben forgave me,
but I knew I needed
to search for the something
that was worth
forgiving

in myself.

"I hope you find
What you're looking for
at Princeton,"
Jordan said,
wiping his eyes.

"I'm not going either,"
I responded.
The salty tears started to dry
on my cheeks.

He cocked his head.
"Where are you going?"

"Nowhere.
Well, not nowhere.
China, probably."

Jordan gave me a look
like he didn't understand.

"I'm taking a gap year,"
I continued.

"My father has a six-month project
in Shanghai next fall,

500 Words or Less   357

so we are all going to move there
with him.

"And my stepmother
used to own an art gallery.
She's going to try
to get me an internship."

I'd had no idea Xiaoling
was a former gallery owner.

There were so many things
I didn't know
about the people
around me.
About my family.
About myself.

"What about your mom?
Is she back?
I thought I saw her
at Starbucks the other day."

"Sort of.
She lives in Portland
with my aunt.
But she's here for graduation."

Jordan nodded.
"How is she?"

"All right.
She has a job.
She quit drinking.
I have her phone number.
It's progress."

Jordan reached out
and grasped my shoulder.
"Progress is
everything."

Then he zipped up
his backpack
with everything
tucked back inside,
removed his sunglasses,
and stepped into class.

I thought I cheated on Ben

Because I was young and
flippant and
careless.

Because I was selfish
and self-involved.

I thought I cheated on Ben
because I could.

We could do anything.

We dug holes
too deep,
jumped off
too many cliffs,
got caught
in too many avalanches.

We lived and lived
like yesterday was the end,
until one day you woke up
and it was.

But I cheated on Ben
because

I never saw him
for who he was.

I never looked him in the eye
long enough
to know him
like I knew myself,

because I never looked at myself
long enough
to know
who I was.

So how are you supposed to
dig yourself out
of your own snowy grave?

You just are,
with your hands
and your feet
and your heart
melting into puddles.

Burial

There was a piece of me left
in the ground.
There was the grade-school me,
when Ben and I were friends.
The high school me,
when we were more than friends.
The cheater me.
The insecure me.
The rotten me.
And somewhere in that plot of ground
there were seeds growing
a new part of me.

Sandwiches
Kitty and Ashok
sat together
at a picnic table
in the courtyard
outside the AP Bio classroom.

I saw them
and they saw me
and most of me
thought about
continuing to walk right by.

"'Sup, girl,"
Ashok said,
and I froze.

I wanted to unravel
everything I held
so tightly inside.

"I'm sorry," I said.

They both stopped eating,
and Kitty turned around
to face me.

"I've been a shitty friend!"

"Yep," Kitty said, but she smiled.
"Come sit with us."

I squeezed in next to Kitty
and emptied the contents
of my lunch sack onto the table.

A roasted turkey sandwich
with avocado, tomatoes,
and a chipotle aioli sauce
on a crusty French baguette.

Ashok and Kitty
both stared.

"Did you make that?"
Kitty asked.

"Yeah."

"It's not smashed.
Your sandwiches are always
smashed,"
Kitty said.

"Why the change?"
Ashok asked.

I shrugged.
"I wanted to try something new."
I bit into the sandwich.

Sauce and turkey and bits of avocado
dribbled down my chin.

Kitty and Ashok
both reached inside their bags.
They pulled out extra napkins.

"Here," they said in unison.

I wiped away
the particles of food,
the sauce,
the messiness
of life itself,

and cleaned myself up
at least for the time being,

until the next time
we eat sandwiches

and bits of food
and sauce
dribble down our faces.

Through a mouth full of food
I said,
"So, tell me, what's new
with you?"

In the end

At Meydenbauer,
we were imperfect.
We were lost.
We were, at times,
careless, selfish,
stubborn,
and scared.

But in the end,
we left those selves
behind,

sitting in a chair in a classroom,
stuffed into a locker,
stranded on a bleacher.

There was no room
for the self I had carried
through high school,
in the bags I packed,
headed, not to Princeton,
not to college,

headed somewhere
in a car

parked in the East parking lot
after seventh period
on the last day of high school.

In the end,
I wanted to feel
like I could leave this place
with some semblance of solace.

I wanted to feel like
maybe I was on a process
to wholeness.

We were all
about to walk
away from Meydenbauer,

beyond our worlds
of a life distilled
into five hundred words or less.

We were all
disassembled parts
waiting to become
whole.

We were infinite pages
of letters and words
waiting to be written.

We were human.
We were alive.

Acknowledgments

So grateful to my agent, Brent Taylor, for believing in novels written in verse, for seeing a special place for this story in the world, and for being an outstanding champion of my work. Seriously, best agent ever.

Immense gratitude to my editor, Jennifer Ung. I am so honored to be among your list of authors. Thank you for being so dedicated to the voices, stories, and work of under-represented authors, in particular authors of color. The publishing world is a better place because of you and your work.

Thank you to everyone at Simon Pulse for supporting verse novels and this book. Thank you to Sarah Creech for the beautifully designed cover, and thank you to Cannaday Chapman for the gorgeous illustration.

Thank you to everyone at Triada US Literary Agency for the support and enthusiasm for my work.

My sincerest gratitude to my incredible critique partners who have spent years reading drafts and providing constructive feedback. We did this together, and I am a better writer because of all of you.

To the Longmont ladies—Penny, Eileen, Leslie, Stephanie, and Susan (as listed in couch order, clockwise—Ha!): thank you so much for inviting me into your group. I am so honored to be able to work with all of you. And thank you for continuing to remind me that "it's a nickel for every word you use."

To the Seattle folks—Ron, Carol, Corbet, Russell, and Gayle: seven years and counting! Thank you for being the first readers of the "verse version" and seeing something worth pursuing.

Also, a shout-out to Kasie, who served as an accountability partner in the early stages of writing this novel.

To my librarian friends, particularly my friends and colleagues in academic libraries: let's keep making the world a place where stories can thrive, knowledge is created, and everyone has access to both.

To my dear friends in Colorado, in Seattle, from college, and all of you scattered about the world: thank you for all the support and for being just so darn excited to read this book.

To my parents: thank you for all the times you drove us to the library as kids, for being a family that reads, and for all the love and support. To my sister: thank you for teaching me about art and the creative process, and the discipline to make something special.

To Steve: thank you for listening to me ponder nuanced grammar questions, supporting me in finding the space and time to write, and making me coffee with lots of extra foam.

Juleah del Rosario wants you to know that she grew up outside of Seattle in the Eastside. She currently lives a book- and mountain-filled existence as a librarian in Colorado. She is Chamorro and Filipina. Most importantly, she wants you to know that you are loved and you are whole.